From inside the novel...

They paused and sat down. Everyone was exhausted. It was slow going in the dark, and the hike from the car had been mostly uphill. Dewey knew that it would be even steeper after the bridge. He watched as the mayor sat down next to Bibi. Felt a pang of jealousy.

"So you see, Miss Bibi, today we have been killing as many of our elderly as possible. They are not allowed to fight back. They can only hide, or shelter in a field at the top of the mountain. But tomorrow, the tables are turned. They are allowed to kill the adults below the age of sixty. And we are not allowed to fight back. Nor can we use weapons. There is also the fact that we are outnumbered."

"By how many?" asked Bibi.

"Easily four or five to one," said Dewey.

"The only way to survive is to get back to the town of Kita-Yamanouchi. That is our safe area. We begin the march again at dawn. So you see, searching for you is robbing us of precious time."

"Then why don't you have it at night?" asked Bibi. A perfectly obvious question.

"Too dangerous," said the mayor. "Someone could get injured. Or fall off a cliff."

In a small town in northern Japan they celebrate the first national holidays of spring a little differently... a little deadlier... than everywhere else...

Dewey Lane is sick of being an English teacher in Japan. His beautiful Swedish girlfriend has just dumped him for a Tokyo banker. But he's already paid for a vacation with his ex and her friends—to a famous hot spring resort, deep in the Japanese countryside. Waiting for the girls to arrive, he discovers the town is celebrating their first annual "Two Day March."

The longer Dewey stays, however, the more he learns about the event's sinister nature. Day one is euthanasia day—where the young have at the old, taking out the weak, the senile, and the embittered. But on day two, the elderly take revenge...with their own brand of homicidal traditional justice!

THE TWO DAY MARCH

SHANE O'BRIEN MACDONALD

Ankerville Street Productions
North America

First digital edition November 2014
ISBN: 978-0-9939323-0-4
First trade paperback edition November 2014
ISBN: 978-0-9939323-1-1

Found an error in one of our books? Don't get angry, get us to fix it! Contact us:
Ankerville Street Productions North America
ankervillestreetprods@gmail.com

Cover design by Yukiko Sato

PART ONE

THE MONDAY BEFORE GOLDEN WEEK

1

The guy was twitching. He'd boarded about thirty minutes ago. At some out-of-the-way station at the edge of an out-of-the-way farming community. After a brief glance at the other passengers in the car, he headed straight for Dewey.

The only white person in sight.

There were plenty other vacant seats on the train. The compartment was far from even a quarter full. Certainly nothing like Dewey had grown accustomed to in Tokyo. But it was a given that the guy was going to ask for English lessons. Or he would open a textbook, and causally approach Dewey with a question about grammar. It had happened before. And always on a rural train line. It would happen, of course, in the most awkward manner possible.

One of Dewey's Danish coworkers, despite the fact he spoke English in a manner indistinguishable from a North

American, became monolingual on such occasions. It was just reality that all Japanese people assumed every white person was an American.

But this guy was worse. He twitched.

At first it was just the nervous left leg, bobbing up and down. Then both legs started. A perfunctory interview couldn't be far off now.

When Dewey had first come to Japan, his company had trained him on Japanese culture. Restless legs were a definite no-no. Especially around a stranger. So Dewey could only conclude that the guy next to him was either mentally ill or really didn't like him. It was the guy's way of making a statement without saying anything.

Dewey Lane was only thirty-one years old, but he had sat next to all different kinds of Japanese people. Who had exhibited all kinds of strange behaviors in the presence of a foreign person. Actually, it wasn't that he was a foreign, but that he was…visibly foreign. Clearly A WHITE PERSON. Most Japanese people would only get nervous around another Asian person once they started to speak. Only once hearing the tones of Chinese, Korean, or some other language from further south along the Pacific Rim. Or Mongolia.

One night Dewey had been heading back on the Hibiya line from Ginza, in Tokyo. The only place to stand was in front of a fat, dweeby-looking guy. Who spent the entire trip picking his nose and eating it. Then there were the numerous number of people who simply got up and walked away the moment a white person sat next to them. Or the people, usually on the Saikyo Line, and other trains heading north out of Tokyo, who felt the need the turn on their cell phone's television application and watch it, at high volume, without headphones.

4

A few years earlier, the Japanese companies who made mobile phones—which only functioned with the Japanese cell network—had developed the TV feature. To watch over-the-air broadcasts on the go. It had been hugely popular. For exactly three and a half months. Then Dewey never saw a single person doing it. Except as a non-verbal protest against Dewey's presence.

Then there was the schoolgirl, outside Ofuna on the Tokkaido Line, probably about fourteen, who spent twenty-five minutes looking at him in awe, like she'd seen a god. Of course, that had been his interpretation of her unending gaze.

Dewey looked over an caught sight of the guy's clothes. He was dressed in an AKB48 T-shirt. Appropriate for this kind of weather. The man's skin was covered with blotches of red. Rashes and infections everywhere.

He had been told, with great authority by Yuko, one of his coworkers in Shinjuku, that thirty per cent of all Japanese had some form of skin disease. Of course, most never got it treated. To see a doctor meant they had to pay thirty per cent of the bill. If they had a job of some sort. Many unemployed didn't bother paying their government health insurance bill. Since there was no legal way to compel them to pay for the government insurance.

Which meant they couldn't go to a hospital. You were only compelled to pay for insurance if you worked more than thirty hours a week, with your employer paying half. If you worked less, you had to buy a different kind of insurance, called 'citizens health insurance.' Which got quite a bit more expensive after a few years, with premiums that always went up for reasons Dewey couldn't explain.

The bottom line was many people in Japan didn't go to the doctor, almost all of them poor. So on trains, especially outside central Tokyo, people tended to look a lot rougher. It was almost the opposite of the United States, where the destitute were gathered in the inner cities, close to shelters and charities. He always heard the Brits and Canadians complaining about rough looking Japanese.

Dewey had at least been able to score a window seat. On the local trains there was no reserved seating. They were traveling right along the ocean. The wrong side of Japan, as they called it in Tokyo and Osaka. The Sea of Japan side. It wasn't really fair to say this. Just that, coincidentally, all the cities with most of the country's wealth were on the Pacific side.

The weather was a lot worse along the Sea of Japan. Along Honshu and Kyushu they weren't spared the disgusting humid summers that prevailed from June to early September. Despite this, these same places suffered a far worse winter. Cold Siberian winds passed over the sea, collecting moisture. When this mass of cold, wet air hit the mountains in central Japan, they released the moisture as snow, blanketing the northwest coast. Before continuing on as cold, dry air to the other side of the country. While the Pacific coast might see little more than flurries once or twice a winter, the Sea of Japan often saw accumulations of several meters of wet snow. Enough to make life miserable.

Still, it was an incredible place to travel by train. The train tracks were carved into the side of a cliff. Occasionally passing by a lonely house, where some brave soul had decided to tough it out. From Dewey's window it was straight drop to the sea. Looking down he could only see water. Of course, the view of the horizon was obscured by giant pillars. Upon which rested the Hokuriku Expressway. Rising out of the ocean on concrete pylons. Dewey wondered what would happen if a major quake struck. You'd have no place to jump, except the ocean.

An earthquake had struck, about ten years earlier, in Niigata. Almost took out the nuclear power plant. Japan seemed to enjoy rolling the dice when it came to atomic energy. All in a bid for increased self sufficiency. That was how the country operated, thought Dewey, keep doing what you're doing until you walk right into catastrophe.

Staring out at the sea, Dewey wondered if they'd passed into Yamagata from Niigata prefecture. The route he'd planned wouldn't take him to Yamagata city, so there was no way of knowing. It would still be several hours to Akita, to the hot spring town.

Another house caught Dewey's eye. A brightly colored chalet, looking like it had been transplanted from the Alps of Switzerland. His glance drifted to the twitchy guy. Their eyes met briefly, then Dewey looked away. The man had angry eyes. He looked down at the man's sweatpants. Country clothing for the rural poor. The man had a small backpack by his feet.

Dewey felt needling in his right abdomen. Twitchy guy's elbow. The train turned away from the sea, towards a valley of rice fields. They passed through a tunnel. The elbowing got worse. Was this the guy's protest against Dewey's presence? The man could have sat anywhere.

Finally Dewey couldn't stand it anymore. "Excuse me," he said in Japanese, "could you please put your elbow down?" He pointed to his waist. "You're hitting me right here. Stop, please."

7

The guy immediately retracted his arms. Dewey's foreign language ability was far from perfect, but it had done the job. The guy hadn't expected the foreigner to say anything, let alone in Japanese. Dewey had noticed such behavior in his four years living in Tokyo. People often felt free to behave badly because most Japanese, at least in East Japan, put up with them, or tried to ignore such transgressions.

Then the muttering started. Rapid-fire. Like a whisper, under twitchy guy's breath. Like he was chanting. Dewey looked over. The guy's eyes were closed. It was really creepy. Dewey tried to lean towards the window, as far away as possible. Letting the sound of the tracks drown everything else out.

Just when Dewey felt he could no longer bear it, twitchy guy got up and left. For the moment. Dewey noticed he'd left his backpack behind. The train emerged from the tunnel. Rice fields all around. The announcement for the next station came on.

A rush of air blew through the compartment. Someone had opened both doors connecting the train cars.

From above came a bunch of clomps. Like a horse was walking on the top of the train.

They hit a straightaway. The train slowed abruptly. An automated announcement came on in Japanese. Dewey couldn't really understand it, because he'd only heard it twice before, in his entire four years living here. But he was pretty sure what it was before the chipper female voice came on in English: "The emergency brakes have been applied. Please grab hold of a hand strap or railing to prevent injury from sudden deceleration."

Someone had jumped in front of the train.

They would be here for a while. Waiting for the police to arrive.

2

Every seat on the Yamagata shinkansen had been booked. The Joetsu one, too. In fact, all the bullet trains heading to Hokuriku were reserved well in advance. Which came as a shock to Dewey. Those two lines, along with the Akita and Yamagata shinkansens, were regarded as the white elephants of Japanese infrastructure. Built during the eighties when Japan was rolling in it. The government doubled down. The Niigata shinkansen would open soon, completing a loop of money-losing high-speed train service to places no one wanted to go.

And yet, they were booked solid for all of Golden Week. To understand why, it has to be known that the entire country of Japan goes on vacation at the same time. A cultural shock to most Americans. There were three main travel periods. New Year's, which went from the first of January to the first Monday of the following week. Unlike North Americans, most Japanese treat Christmas as a holiday to see one's boyfriend or girlfriend, while New Year's Day is considered more solemn, and reserved for family activities.

After that came Golden Week—three consecutive statutory holidays, with a fourth that fell with a workday between it and the other three. At Dewey's company the language instructors got the entire week off. Fortunately.

Then, in the middle of August came obon (pronounced OH-BONE, something that took Dewey years to master). While there were no statutory holidays on the calendar, virtually the entire country took at least a week off in the middle of the month.

During these periods all flights, trains and highways were packed. Even money losing routes like the Joetsu and Nagano shinkansen. Hell, they weren't even proper bullet trains. They ran on conventional rails, just a little bit faster, unlike the Tokkaido line, which was grade separated on special tracks. And the Joetsu line didn't even go to Joetsu. It stopped at Niigata city.

Dewey started out his widow. In the distance he caught a glimpse of flashing red lights. The police were on the scene now. This sort of thing happened every week in Tokyo. There were even times, often near the bi-yearly bonus seasons, when trains were stopped every day. By "human body fall accidents." Salarymen jumping to claim life insurance for their families. Some of the private train companies had gotten wise to this and started going after the families of suicide victims. Compensation for the costs in delays and clean up.

Dewey had been delayed no less than five times by jumper in the last eight months. Usually on a Wednesday, just after lunch. People just couldn't hack it. Isolated and alone. Couldn't make it to the weekend. Lunch in Japan is a full hour, by law, at all companies. A time when coworkers socialize and gossip. The embarrassment of not belonging to a group has driven some employees, and often university students, to have their lunches in bathroom stalls. To avoid the stigma of eating alone. Some don't make it back to work, preferring hara-kiri by rail line and rolling stock.

Then there was the salaryman who had jumped in front of a Marunochi line train one afternoon. In a spectacularly ill-timed attempt, this individual had bounced off the front car of the train. His entire weight bounced back onto the platform, nailing an innocent bystander full bore. Dewey didn't know if the person on the platform had lived or not.

Feeling a bit hungry, Dewey reached up and grabbed his backpack. He had stuffed it full with toiletries and clothing. An attempt to pack as lightly as possible. In the front compartment he found a small plastic bag from 7-11. Inside, a bottle of green tea and a package of dried squid strips. While they had potato chips and chocolate bars, Dewey had gone to the effort of consuming local snacks. The green tea was sugarless, naturally almost free of calories.

He'd arrived in Osaka two nights previous. With all the trains booked, he'd bought a seishin jyuuhachi kippu (pronounced SAY-SHIN-JEW-HA-CHEE…oh, fuck it. It's not important), a long-winded name for a train ticket that made far more sense in the original kanji. It allowed a full day's travel on any local train run by Japan Railways.

Unfortunately that meant no shinkansens or reserved seats. But you got five days of travel, which you could share with friends. All for little more than twenty dollars a day. A pretty good deal.

On the second day, Dewey made his way to Niigata. Despite have a population of over three quarters of a million people, it had made almost no impression on him. If you had to pick a generic place in Japan, you could do no more unremarkable than Niigata City. The usual collection of overpriced department stores. Hocking luxury handbags. The usual chains of izakayas, coffee shops, and fast food restaurants. Although Dewey had heard the sake was quite good. Ample access to rice and decent water.

On his way there Dewey had a layover for half an hour in Joetsu. It was probably the most depressing place he'd ever been. A crumbling town of old buildings and even older people. What is this country going to do? he wondered. The elderly were a financial time bomb. The countryside was hollowing out. Soon every city of less than two million people was going to look like Joetsu. Ugly wooden buildings slowly being ravaged away by the elements.

It was the kind of thing that dissuaded Dewey from putting down roots here.

He'd started working for the ABC Language Academy four years ago. They almost never gave much of a raise, but they were generous in allotting more vacation days the longer you stayed. Which, in some ways, was better.

In Japan both the school and work years start at the beginning of April. Despite the recent push to change them to September. So you began a new schedule of classes, and within a month you had a vacation—Golden Week. So named by movie theater owners after the golden profits the statutory holidays delivered. If the spring holidays fell on the right days, as they did this year, people would end up with an entire week off. Most years people went back to work for a day after the first holiday, then got three more days to hit the road. Now people were pushing to add a forth day. Make it a full week every year.

Despite getting some extra vacation time this year, Dewey's vacation was, unfortunately, doomed. Bibi and everything else going on was making Dewey miserable. How had things gotten this way? He wasn't a weak man. The wrong girl had come into his life. Now said girl was gone. Until this trip. Because of workplace bullshit. He should have gone to Hawaii.

Something caught his attention outside. Two police. Carrying a stretcher, draped in a blue tarp. Walking on the narrow embankment by the tracks.

The man carrying the front end of the stretcher slipped.

The tarp fell off, revealing a mass of red and black. Something rolled off, like a basketball, coming to rest below Dewey's window.

The basketball had a face.

The twitchy guy. The train had cut his head clean off.

3

Two hours later, the train resumed its journey.

According to one of Dewey's colleagues in Tokyo, the police had to identify and mark the location of each piece of human remains. Just in case it turned out not to be a suicide. Although Dewey had never heard of that happening. In the capital region, investigators had it down pat, clearing a site in about forty minutes. But this wasn't Tokyo.

Dewey finished off his squid strips, and hungered for more. Regretted not buying an onigiri or a sandwich.

The next section of the journey took Dewey away from the ocean. Past endless rice fields. Watching the entirety of the country's staple sustenance fly by. Japan imported plenty of food, but not rice. And the government paid farmers real well to maintain that supply. It was a long journey, with many unexpected stops now that the schedule was disrupted. Hours later the train pulled in to Sakata station in Akita.

It was a forty-five minute wait for the train to Kita-Yamanouchi. Dewey was starving. Walking through town, he passed by nothing but abandoned stores. Long since closed down. He headed back to the station. In the convenience store next to the waiting room he found nothing left on the refrigerated shelves but a lone egg salad sandwich. It would have to do.

The final departure of the day was a small two-car train that looked about eighty years old. He really was heading to the edge of civilization. A far cry from the ten-car trains of the Yamanote Line. At least it wasn't crowded. He counted no more than half a dozen people on board. Weathered farmers and a couple of school children. The train only ran seven times each day. Dewey was lucky he hadn't missed it.

As night fell, his cell phone's battery died. Dewey had three more hours to go. He fell asleep. When he awoke the train was almost there, pulling into the second-last station. After departing they entered a tunnel for the final leg of the journey. It must have taken twenty minutes to pass through it all. In Japan this wasn't unusual. It reminded him of the train heading into Nagasaki. The feeling of a place cut off from the rest of the world. Almost.

Kita-Yamanouchi. "Kita" as in north. "Yama" meant mountain. "no" was the connecting particle. "uchi" was Japanese for innermost. This place must be inside the mountains. But as the train came to rest at the final stop, the first thing Dewey saw out his window was a harbor. Strange. He hadn't expected to be so close to the water.

Dewey disembarked. He was the only passenger who wasn't a high school student. Out beyond the platform was a small village. Nestled in darkness. He looked up at the platform clock. Five minutes after ten. Late. Dewey took out his wallet. He needed money. All he had left was the equivalent of thirty-five dollars in cash.

He found a 7-11 next to the station. Went right up to the ATM. After checking that it did, in fact, take Mitsubishi-UFJ bank cards, he attempted to make a withdrawal. He was then greeted by a message that informed him the machine was only operational between the hours of eight in the morning until ten at night.

Dewey was in trouble. He had no money. And he had no map. After wandering the streets for fifteen minutes, he found the Yamanoki Ryokan. This was where Megumi had booked them in. He walked into the genkan. The place looked dark the only sign of life the far off noise of a television. Dewey knocked on the wall next to the shelves where people put their shoes.

"Hello?" he yelled in English.

A figure appeared at the end of the hall. "Good evening," said the aging woman in Japanese.

Dewey switched languages. "I'm really sorry I'm late." He explained his situation on the train.

"Yes," said the women, "It is regrettable, but we cancel reservations after nine o'clock. The only room we have left is the larger one. Unfortunately it costs a great deal more."

"Yes," he said, "but I might have a problem paying." He explained about his bank card. "But I'll give you cash first thing tomorrow morning."

"Do you have a credit card?"

"Not one that works in Japan."

By the woman's silence Dewey gathered that she was pissed. But it wouldn't be good manners to turn him out on the street. There were no other hotels or hostels in the village. It was this place or a bench on the train platform.

After a long awkward pause she nodded and beckoned him in. He was led down a narrow hallway. Then up to an enormous second floor room. It could have slept an entire family, easily.

"How much is this?" he asked.

She quoted him a number that was more than a third of the monthly rent on his Tokyo apartment.

Dewey nodded. "What other choice did he have?" There went his savings. "Is there anyway I could order something to eat?"

"I'm sorry," she said, "but we've finished dinner service."

After an awkward pause, with which Dewey realized that getting information out of this women would be like pulling teeth, he asked, "Is there any place around here that serves food?"

"There is an izakaya next door."

"Thank you."

After settling in, Dewey went out to examine the town. The placed next door turned out to be a yakitori restaurant. He was too tired to guess what the strange kanjis on the menu meant, so he continued on.

Everything on the main street was closed. Not a surprise. In many of these country places, everything shuts down at six o'clock. Dewey turned the corner by the train station.

Right above him was an illuminated sign. An authentic Irish pub. In the middle of nowhere. And it was open. Unbelievable.

The interior was a perfect imitation. And completely deserted. From the kitchen he heard someone greeting him in Japanese. The moment the man saw Dewey, he switched to English. "What can I get for you?"

"You speak English," said Dewey.

"Of course, everyone in this town speaks it perfectly. It's the law."

4

You're joking," said Dewey.

"No," said the man. "It is all to attract more tourists to our village. We got a special loan to open this bar."

Dewey looked around. "It's very authentic."

"Will you have drink?"

"Yes, how about a pint of Rogue Amber?"

"Sure." The bartender grabbed a glass.

"And do you have a food menu?"

"Right here."

"My god," said Dewey, looking at the long list of dishes. "I'll try the haggis."

"A very good choice."

"How long have you studied English for? I've never met anyone who speaks it so well, not even in Roppongi."

The man laughed and passed over the drink. "That's five hundred yen." Dewey passed him a coin. The man yelled into the kitchen in Japanese, then turned back. "Our mayor is very proactive here. He wants to spur economic development. Part of that is making our village more accessible to tourists. He wants to have a one hundred per cent bilingual population in the next five years."

Dewey sipped his beer. "That's quiet ambitious."

"It is. But it's been quite effective so far." The man wiped the bar. "Also, this week is one of our major events."

"What's that?"

"The two day march."

"Oh yeah, I've heard of those. Kind of like a marathon, right?"

"Something like that. Will you be here for a while?"

"Yeah. Until next week."

"I see." The bartender poured himself a small draft of beer. "What do you do in Tokyo?"

"I'm an English teacher."

The bartender smiled. Dewey expected that most foreigners who came in here said the same thing. "You work at an eikaiwa?"

"Yes. The ABC Language Academy. You've heard of it?"

The man nodded. "One of my friends took lessons there as a child."

"Did they learn much?"

"Nope. Nothing."

"Yeah, it's pretty much useless for most of the people who come through the door. There's no way you're going to learn anything if you come in once or twice a week. I guess they see it as a hobby. I also teach at a women's university twice a week."

"Lots of pretty girls."

"You'd think, but it feels a lot like a glorified high school. I mean, the girls are nice. But they all seem the blend into one big mass of females. I like to be with a girl who stands out."

"Do you like Japanese girls?"

"Sure. But I don't think they like me."

The bartender laughed. "Some girls are very difficult. Many can get money by working at a hostess club."

"Yeah," said Dewey, "that would never fly back home. In America the only people who are paid to look pretty are models and prostitutes."

"But the little cute girls? They look innocent, but they are not. Many of them like to have sex."

"I'll bet." Dewey mused that a tall girl wouldn't have many potential suitors in Japan.

"So," asked the bartender, "why did you come to Japan?"

Ahh, thought Dewey, the inescapable question at every first encounter with a Japanese person. He at least gave the guy credit for taking so long to get to it. Usually it was the first question he was asked. Then the one about Japanese girls. "Well," said Dewey, finishing his drink and indicating his desire for another one, "I moved back to Santa Barbara after college. Couldn't find any jobs in finance. So I decided to come here. That was right after the financial crisis. Been here for four years."

"Do you want to stay here?"

"Not sure. Hard to make money living in Tokyo, the cost of rent is high."

The bartender approached with another pint of beer.

Dewey couldn't believe it was so cheap. "Another Rogue Amber." He took the 500 yen coin. "How is it?"

"Excellent. I can't believe you have all these beers on tap."

"It's our specialty. Many Americans come here for it. Some from as far away as Sendai and Aomori. Many of them are English teachers."

"Yeah. It's not a very good job if you like money. But you get a lot of free time. I feel bad for those salarymen who have to work really hard, but get only one day a week off. It must be awful."

"It is. I used to be one of those," said the bartender. "Every day I would work from eight-thirty in the morning until midnight. And on two Saturdays every month."

"Yeah, you never see that in America."

The bartender smiled. "There is an American who comes in here many nights."

"Oh yeah? Where's he from?"

"Texas, I believe."

"Yeah, the U.S. has really gone to the dogs. Ever since Obama got in. He's the one who caused all this mess. After all those people fighting in Iraq. This is their reward. I think Rand Paul is our only hope. He knows what's going on. I'm willing to bet he'll be the next president."

"Why? Do you like President Bush?"

"Hell no. He was stupid. Spending all this money on his friends. Telling everyone what to do. Looking through library books to catch terrorists. And for what? They found two guys in ten years. But every bureaucrat and cop loves him. Every single one got a boost in salary. Spending their time pretending to look for terrorists. My ass!"

"Bush was not popular in Japan. People like Obama because in Fukui—"

"Yeah, I passed through the town yesterday."

"Did you try the Echizen soba? It is very famous."

"No, maybe next time."

A bell rang. The bartender grabbed Dewey's dinner from the kitchen. The plate was steaming hot. Dewey had never had haggis before. It was like a kind of meatloaf, except spicy. A bit dry, but it was good.

When Dewey was done eating the bartender approached. "You should come to the march on Friday."

"I don't know. My traveling companions are arriving that afternoon."

"Really? Other teachers?"

"One of them. The other two are eikaiwa staff. All girls."

"How exciting. Do they like to go hiking?"

"No idea. I doubt they Japanese girls are into it. They seemed excited to come visit the onsen. Don't know about the other one."

"Is she American, too?"

"Nope. Swedish."

"A blond girl?"

"Very blond."

Is she your girlfriend?

Dewey paused. This was awkward. "No. She likes to date Japanese guys. Likes their skin."

The bartender laughed. "You should hook up me."

"Hook you up? Sure. I'm more gunning for her Japanese friend anyway."

PART TWO

THE PREVIOUS JANUARY

5

The platform was packed with people. All heading home.

Bibi Anderson hated long train rides. It was why she moved to Gakugei-Daigaku. The Toyoko Line was less than ten minutes by express to Shibuya and the Yamanote Line connection. And the local train turned into the Hibiya Metro Line, so she could get across town to Ginza without making any changes. After surviving her first broiling summer in Tokyo last year, she learned what the rest of the locals knew: changing trains is what kills you. Gakugei was close enough to everything that she didn't have to worry if she stayed out late, but it was also residential enough to be a nice place to live. People didn't go there unless they needed to. Which kept it from getting too crowded.

So, when Kishimoto-san had asked her to take over the shift in Saitama, Bibi had almost said no. Saitama was the prefecture on the northern border of Tokyo. A suburb. Much like Yokohama to the southwest, except without the charm of a seaport and a fancy Chinatown. Saitama was, however, famous for having Japan's largest shopping mall. And for being a good place to own a car. Bibi's commute took her to Shibuya station, then down a long corridor connecting to the Saikyo Line platform. Saikyo—a combination of Saitama and Tokyo. It made a lot more sense if you could read Japanese.

"It's known as the chikan-sen," said Megumi, Bibi's co-worker at Shinjuku station.

Bibi searched her limited Japanese vocabulary. "Uh-huh? Is that good?"

Megumi smiled. "It's the pervert line. Chikan—pervert. Man who touches a woman's body when she doesn't like it."

"Oh."

"Many men go on the internet and plan to touch women together."

"I see."

It was only for three weeks. There weren't that many students in Saitama who needed to learn Swedish or German, the languages Bibi taught. But it meant that her day was stretched out. The ABC English Corporation had schools all over the Tokyo area, but Bibi usually only taught in locations stretching between Ginza and Yokohama. Urban areas. Mostly businessmen and exchange students. Saitama was an anomaly. They had a German instructor who would take over at the end of the month. But until then, it meant an hour and ten minutes on a train. Closer to an hour and a half once walking to the station was taken into account.

With that in mind on her first day taking over the shift, Bibi squeezed onto an overcrowded commuter train at Shibuya. The doors closed and they departed. The Saikyo Line by-passed more than half of the Yamanote line stations. Giving the illusion of moving fast. But at each stop the overcrowded train took on more and more passengers. It was now about a quarter to seven at night. Plenty of people, especially women, were now off work.

After they departed Ikebukuro station, Bibi felt something on her ass. At first she thought it was the normal crush of passengers, but the pressure moved up her abdomen. To her right breast, below where her raised arm clutched the hand strap.

Someone had their hand on her.

Bibi snapped around. The hand disappeared. Behind her was a skinny young man in a suit and tie. She stared at him long and hard, but he looked in the other direction. When he finally turned around, their eyes met. He gazed at her almost defiantly.

She turned back towards the door, angry that the man had acted so cowardly. No apology. I mean, he'd been caught, she thought.

Then she felt stroking on her thigh. What was she to do? Yell for help? No one on the train probably spoke English. The man felt upwards, to her crotch. She was about to swat him away, when she did something she never expected.

She relaxed.

The train pulled into Akabane Station. Bibi was pushed out the door as people exited the train, the young man in the suit with them.

The train continued on. Twenty or so minutes later they arrived at Musashi-Uruwa. Bibi walked to the school, troubled by her reaction. Everything in her being said she should've chased after the guy. Taken him to the police. But she didn't feel fear. She felt…uncomfortably good. It was like her brain and her body were saying two different things.

She arrived at work and put it all behind her. Her student was a young woman whose husband was from Sweden. They would be visiting Stockholm in August. Bibi taught her some useful idioms and gave her helpful travel advice in English. Then went home around nine-thirty. The Saikyo Line into Tokyo was almost empty, save for a sprinkling of people on the bench seats. She listened to a Japanese podcast for English speakers and glanced at the faces of other people on the train. Something in her longed for the crowded tension of the trip earlier.

Then Bibi put all this out of her mind. Until three weeks later. She sat in the Doutour café in Ebisu Garden Place. It was packed. Two young men were talking, both Japanese businessmen. She noticed the salaryman opposite her was cute, and very well dressed in a tie that coordinated well with his shirt. After gazing at him for a few minutes, the alarm on her phone went off.

The Saikyo Line stopped in Ebisu, taking her direct to her last class in Saitama. The setting sun beat down on her as she crossed the piazza. Bibi felt a bit sweaty as she boarded the train. Made only worse by the fact that they had the heat on, despite the relatively warm winter day. The train was pretty empty. She noticed the guy from the café. He boarded and stood right next to her.

Over the next three stops the train got more and more crowded. Bibi grabbed a hand towel from her purse to dab the sweat off her neck. The guy in the suit was pressed up against her body as she unbuttoned her blouse and dabbed at her breasts, the tops of which were now exposed. The whole trip to Saitama she felt her nipples rub up against the guy's chest. Just before they got to Musashi-Urawa station, she felt his hand brush up against her bosom.

Then the train pulled into the station. She smiled at him. He rushed ahead of her. She followed him out as far as the bicycle garage, then turned around, buttoning up her blouse.

The whole trip home she couldn't get his face out of her mind. Wishing his hands had gone further, caressing her body. Two strangers in a crowd.

The train pulled into Shibuya station. Bibi headed up, but instead of going straight to the Tokyu Line which would take her to Gakugei-Daigaku, she decided to wander around for a while. She headed up past the 109 department store, into the crowds and the bright lights. She took a left and headed down an alleyway. To her right she saw a sign with a picture of a vibrator on it. Scanning the street for someone who might recognize her, she ducked down a stairwell.

The store was mostly empty, except for two young businessmen and a couple, all of whom ignored her.

She walked up to a display of vibrators. Inspected several models, all of which looked oversized for her needs. Next to them were a line of vibrating eggs. That, to Bibi, seemed far more practical. Despite the fact that she felt confident in her sexual history, she'd never owned a stimulation device of her own. A boy she'd dated at twenty-one, just for three months, had once tried to get her to play with one that he'd bought for her. She'd feigned interest until his requests began to make her uncomfortable. Shortly after she stopped replying to his text messages.

Impulsively she grabbed a purple egg and walked up to the counter. Paid in cash. Walked out ignoring the other customers.

An hour later, alone in her room she took the egg out of her bag. Examined the controls. Simple. Bibi put the device on her bedside table and headed off to take a shower.

Later that night she was awoken by her Australian neighbor, Roderick. He had a terrible habit of clomping up the stairs. A woman giggled. Great, thought Bibi, he'd brought another girl home. She heard muffled voices, which half an hour later gave way to serious giggling.

Bibi turned restlessly. Then came a pounding sound from next door. Muffled squeals. Then unmuffled squeals. He must be drunk, they were going at it for quite some time. She reached down, felt herself getting wet. Bibi grabbed the egg, turning it on to a medium setting. It vibrated against her tummy. She pushed it down to her crotch, rubbing it in a circular pattern around her clitoris. Waves of pleasure grew stronger. The moans kept coming from next door. The heavy, standard-issue guest house bed banging against the wall.

She screamed.

Bibi had her first orgasm since the Georgetown International Students Society semi-formal when she was nineteen.

6

The next week, on her day off, Bibi went back to the same Doutour. She stayed in the coffee shop until closing, but she never saw the guy with the stylish tie. She went and sat down on a bench near the downstairs exit of Ebisu station. Time wore on. People must have thought she was insane, sitting around until nearly one in the morning. But she figured many of these Japanese guys were shy. Maybe she needed to be more proactive.

She walked up the hill to Daikanyama station. The last local train departed close to one-thirty. She passed darkened couture clothing stores and small trendy restaurants. Why was she doing this? Dewey was her boyfriend. If she wanted affection she could have called him up.

But then, she was kind of bored with him.

They had met when she was an exchange student in Washington. She was studying applied linguistics at Georgetown. It had been her first time to North America. Washington was dangerous, but seemed to give the impression of power. Like Rome. Lots of money spent on statues and monuments.

At the Georgetown campus Dewey lived on the same floor. They had belonged to the same group of friends who hung out all the time. Partied. A mixture of international students and Americans. She enjoyed Dewey, and the other Californians on campus. They were, for the most part, laid back. The closest you could find to Europeans in the United States. Dewey and Bibi had become good friends. But she still had a boyfriend back in Stockholm. And Dewey just wasn't the kind of person with whom she'd cheat on someone.

Everyone had kept in touch, one of the curses of the modern age. Bibi had gone back to Stockholm and graduated. Started a job at a bank. Something that had absolutely nothing to do with applied linguistics. Dewey had left for Japan. Bibi spent days scrolling her Facebook account learning about Tokyo. Mildly jealous of anyone who got to live overseas. But she counted herself lucky to have a job— far better than most of her friends.

Then the bank was merged. Bibi found herself unemployed. Dewey had mentioned that his company needed a Swedish teacher. It just happened, by coincidence, that Bibi was also fluent in German, which allowed the ABC school to hire her full time. If she would come to Tokyo. She was told, however, that her expectations of life would need some adjustment. At least as far as food and living space were concerned. Bibi didn't care. She wanted adventure.

So, the company had set her up at a guest house in Gakugei-Daigaku. Dewey lived in Sangenjaya, not too far away. They started to hang out together, and he introduced her to the many varieties of Japanese comfort food available at izakayas.

"But you know," Dewey had said, that first night they went for drinks, "my dating life hasn't been all that spectacular."

Bibi smiled, and sipped from a mug of beer. "Why's that?"

"I guess I just expected more action. More romance. But every girl I've dated here has been from some country other than Japan."

"Maybe your language skills need a brush up."

"I know. I'm working on it. I can do basic chit-chat. But I dated a Chinese girl. Than another American. And then a Canadian. Can you believe that? Hard to say that's exotic."

"How are things going with Laurie? She's from…."

"Toronto."

"Yeah. I'd like to visit Canada some time. See the Rockies."

Dewey pressed a button. "I need more alcohol. I was supposed to see her tonight, but the idea fills me with dread."

Bibi was flattered that she'd gotten Dewey's attention. He wasn't the best looking guy, but he was far from the worst. With time, she might get to like him. At least, that was what she had thought.

Since they both had the next day off, they continued drinking well past last train. Dewey had to go back to

Shibuya and transfer. But as the glasses of booze piled up, they hadn't kept an eye on their watches. It was two in the morning before either checked their cell phones.

"I'm completely fucked," Dewey said, outside Gakugei-Daigaku station.

"Well, you can sleep on the floor, next to my bed. If you keep quiet."

"I just need three hours. Then I'll take the first train home."

They stumbled back to the guest house. Dewey took his good old time in the washroom. He came back to the room to find Bibi in her underwear, a sight that had brought a smile to his face. Dewey had crumpled his work pants into a ball to use as a pillow.

"Don't do that," said Bibi.

"But your floor is hard."

"I'll hang them up for you."

"Do you have an extra pillow?" Then Dewey gagged as a drunk Bibi stepped on his stomach. "Watch it."

"At least I didn't trample your groin."

"I wish," he said, punctuating it with a slap to Bibi's behind.

She hung his pants, jacket and shirt, then got under the covers. "Here," she beckoned to him. "You can sleep next to me. But no…."

"No what?" Dewey asked, climbing in.

"Go to sleep."

This lasted about five minutes, before the two of them could no longer resist. They made love. Bibi took delight in screaming extra loudly, to wake up her Australian neighbor.

After that encounter, five months ago, they had started their relationship.

Recently Bibi had grown more distant from him. Probably because they'd started opening up to each other. About things like politics. Bibi found Dewey to be a bit too right-wing for her tastes. He didn't like the idea of public healthcare one bit. Or the metric system.

"Can I ask you something?" he had said to her one evening recently.

"Sure," she said.

"What would you think if I joined the army?"

From then on it was rough going.

7

The truth is, it costs too much for us to go as a couple. All the places with space left are for four or more people. You know, for families."

Bibi was sitting in the break room of the Shinjuku branch of the ABC Language Academy. Looking down over the Lumine department store and the crowds exiting from the south exit of the train station. Next to Yuko, her coworker at the school. They had been discussing Golden Week vacation plans for the past five minutes. Bibi was being a bit disingenuous in her description of the booking situation. There were rooms left for couples. Just not in Kita-Yamanouchi.

"It really is important to Dewey. But don't mention I said that. Would you like to go with us?"

Yuko stared at the wall. Holding back her answer. Despite creeping up on her mid-thirties, she didn't have a boyfriend. So she had no one to go away with. All of her close friends from high school and university were either married or with young children. And she wouldn't dream of vacationing with her mother, who'd already bought a ticket for a flight to Korea over Golden Week. She had been looking forward to having her mother's house in Yokohama to herself.

Still, she like being wanted. And it would give her a chance to brush up on her English.

"How much would it cost?"

Bibi quoted a number that was reasonable, even on Yuko's salary.

The truth was, Bibi would be happy not recruiting vacation buddies. But it was either this, or Dewey would be all over her. With his hands and everything else. At least with the girls sharing a room he couldn't get up to anything funny. With each passing day she felt less interested in him as a lover. Or even as a friend.

"I'll think about it. When do you need to know?"

"Sooner is better," said Bibi. "The thing is, I need to find a fourth person. If you know anyone, that would be a big help."

Yuko thought about the other staff. Megumi had been complaining about how she had set aside her vacation to spend with her boyfriend. But at the last minute he'd agreed to go on a retreat to his boss' house in Atami. She was mighty unhappy to be stuck in Tokyo. And her parents were going away as well, so Megumi had no reason to go back to her hometown in Kyushu.

"I might know someone. Where is the place you want to visit?"

"Kita-Yamanouchi. It's in Akita prefecture."

"I don't know such a place. It's not famous."

"They only have one onsen. They've been doing a lot of advertising on the English-language tourist sites. To bring in more foreign tourists."

"Does the Shinkansen stop there?"

"Actually, no. Just local trains."

"Hmm," said Yuko. "That is difficult. If you have four people you could rent a car. Also, we could spend time camping."

"Really? You can do that? I've never seen any campgrounds in Japan."

"Yes, in the countryside there are many."

Bibi had to start a lesson. They ended the conversation there. Later, as she was finishing, Bibi saw Megumi and Yuko chatting in the office. Whatever Megumi was talking to Yuko about, she seemed eager.

Leaving the office, Bibi headed to Ebisu station. She sat in the coffee shop, reading her book for a couple of hours. Still no sign of the guy with the tie. It was just near closing when she saw HIM walk past, trailing a group of elderly Japanese businessmen. A lightening bolt went through her body. She wanted nothing less than to talk to him. She'd been plotting how to make it happen for weeks now.

Bibi stayed far behind the group. She checked her phone for the Saikyo Line timetable. At this time of night one train stopped at Ebisu every ten minutes on that route. Following the men into the station, she saw the group stop. Some of them were headed for the Yamanote line. Bibi headed to the women's washroom.

She stood in front of the mirror. Checked her makeup. Unbuttoned her blouse, while fastening her suit jacket. This pushed her breasts up. By Japanese standards, enormous breasts. She grabbed two small pads from her bag and carefully placed them in the cup of each bra, elevating each breast. She looked like a floozy in an old Western. It was embarrassing and ridiculous, but there was no way the guy could ignore her now.

Bibi headed down the escalator to the Saikyo Line. The announcement came on for the next train. Where was he? She walked all the way to the last car when she spotted him. He, like every other Japanese man on the platform, had noticed her. As the train rushed by, she lined up behind the tie guy.

The train wasn't that crowded. But all the seats were occupied. She settled in near him, by an exit. After two stops the train was packed. But she couldn't get close enough to the guy. At Ikebukuro station they were both pushed out of the car by exiting passengers. When they moved back on, the two were stuck together like glue. As the train bounced along the tracks, Bibi pressed her chest against him. She moved in a circle. His chin fell against her shoulder. Bibi felt his touch on her waist. She moved his hand up, placing it in her bra. With firmness he touched her skin, her nipples hardening with each sway of the train car.

They reached the next station. Akabane.

The moment was broken.

Again they were pushed out by the exiting crowds, but when she moved back inside, she was separated from the tie guy by a crowd of schoolgirls.

Bibi waited. It was several more stations until they got to Musashi-Uruwa. Bibi got off, heading right for the bicycle garage. But at the bottom of the stairs she turned around. Tie guy was walking down, a few meters behind her.

Now was her chance to make a move.

"Excuse me, could you help? I think I'm lost."

He looked at her awkwardly. Said nothing. Then regained his composure. "Yes, follow me."

Silently she followed him around the station. Then he gestured to a building with a red light on top. A police station. "Over there is the koban. They can help you find the location."

And with that, he left Bibi standing alone, in front of the station.

She'd never felt more disappointed in her life.

8

She had to do it. There was no going back. She had to break up with Dewey. It was a cruel and unusual punishment dragging him along. She couldn't plan a vacation with him. The only way was to dump him now, before money and social capital were invested in the trip to the onsen.

She got to Gakugei-Daigaku and waited. And waited. Some more. Dewey sent her a text saying he was going to be ten minutes late. Bibi considered texting him back with "don't bother, I never want to see you again," but this thought was interrupted by a message from Yuko.

"Megumi will go with us. Are we going to book the onsen?"

"Sure," wrote Bibi. "I'm talking to Dewey in a few minutes."

Things were getting real, weren't they? How could she cancel everything now that two of her co-workers had agreed?

While she was thinking about this, Dewey arrived. With a rose in his hand. "For you, my love."

"How romantic." Bibi faked enthusiasm.

"Are we going to the 270 Yen izakaya?"

"Sure."

They found the basement steps down to the pub and were seated in a booth. Bibi lit up a cigarette as they ordered cocktails. Dewey hated her smoking. She didn't care. "So," she said, looking into his eyes, "you know that hot spring resort you wanted to visit in Akita?"

"Yup."

The next words came out of her mouth completely illogically and inexplicably. Maybe because English was her third language. "I've booked us a room."

"That's great."

"Except...."

"What?"

"They didn't have any double rooms left, so I booked a family-sized room. To cover the costs I invited a couple of the girls from the Shinjuku branch to come with us."

"You mean, other teachers?"

"No, staff."

"Really?" To Dewey this was like inviting people from the planet Mars. "They said yes?"

"Uh-huh. We talked about renting a car, too."

"Why did you book it without asking me?"

"I wanted it to be a surprise."

"And how will we be able to, you know, spend time together?"

"Well, I thought the experience was more important than fucking me. You get to do that three times a week. This is a once in a lifetime opportunity."

"There's no way to cancel?"

"I've already asked the other girls," she lied. "We've all put in a deposit. Megumi put it on her credit card."

"Megumi? And?"

"Yuko."

"She's a nasty skinny bitch."

"Don't say that."

"Well, YOU don't have to work with her."

Bibi put out her cigarette. "You're disappointed."

"I would have liked to talk to them myself. Maybe one of the guys would have gone from my old apartment. Or we could have picked another location."

"I see."

Their drinks arrived. They sipped them in silence.

Eventually Dewey broke and made small talk. Bibi was more worried about what to do than ever. When Dewey was in the toilet she sent a text to Yuko saying the plans were a go. At least she could avoid fucking him on vacation.

She was less lucky when she got back to Dewey's guest house. While she lay on her back and took him inside of her, she fantasized about the man on the train. His touch. In front of strangers.

The next night, after work, she returned to Ebisu. Waiting for him. She saw no sign of tie guy until she walked to the station.

There he was.

It was the exact same time as the previous week. Again they boarded the train together. This time, though, he stayed close to her. And again, between Ikebukuro and Akabane stations, she felt his hands on her body. This time Bibi also touched him, the bulge growing ever-harder underneath the fabric of his pants. He moved his fingers under her skirt, tugging at her pantyhose and underwear. Exploring the moistness running deep inside the warm mass of hair between her legs.

At Akabane he took her hand, leading her out of the station. Bibi had never felt so excited. And afraid. Letting a complete stranger take her. He led her through a maze of houses until they arrived at a park. It was dark, and empty. They found a bench shadowed from the streetlamps by a clump of trees.

He sat her down and undid her blouse, then took off her panties and hosiery. Began to finger her. Rubbing and rubbing until her body convulsed with orgasm. Then she bent down, unzipped his pants, dragged down his underwear, and gave him head. He spurted all over her face, handing her his hand towel to clean up.

Then they buttoned up their clothes, leaving the park hand in hand.

"What's your name?"

"Sato."

"Can you speak English?"

"A little. But I will take classes. For you. What is your name?"

"Bibi."

"You are American?"

"No. Swedish."

Sato stopped, a mischievous grin on his face. "I like Sweden. And Sweden's girls."

Bibi glowed with happiness. She'd just made his night.

Later she got back to her guest house. As she drifted off to sleep she plotted how she was going to break up with Dewey but keep her vacation plans intact.

9

Bibi decided it was better if Dewey dumped her. That way she'd look like the victim. At least in the eyes of her coworkers. The only way she could possibly imagine this working was to get Dewey to cheat on her. Somehow.

She knew the one thing Dewey wanted most was a Japanese girlfriend. He'd hooked up with some Chinese girl his first week here, and had ended up with foreign women ever since.

So Bibi decided to invite Yuko out for drinks with them. Bibi was pretty sure she wasn't dating anyone. They went to an izakaya in a basement under the Kentucky Fried Chicken in Shinjuku.

They discussed plans for half an hour. Bibi had been careful to make sure she was seated across from Yuko and

Dewey, at a table surrounded by high partitions, completely obscured from other patrons. Bibi leaned forward. "I want to see you kiss."

Dewey and Yuko went bug eyed.

"What?" he asked.

"Yeah," said Bibi. "On the lips."

"But he is your boyfriend," said Yuko.

"It's okay. He's never had a Japanese girlfriend. He wants some action."

The next five minutes were spent convincing Bibi that this was a REALLY BAD IDEA. They got the bill. Dewey took Bibi back to Sangenjaya. They fumbled and made love. She didn't really care for it. But she went to bed thinking she'd successfully completed a nuclear strike against their vacation plans.

Then a text arrived from Megumi: "Put the deposit on my credit card. So excited. Will be lot of fun. Shall we rent a car?"

Bibi's stomach sank. The ship had set sail. With two coworkers financially invested, there was no way to get out of their plans.

The next night she met Sato-san in Ikebukuro. They went to a love hotel near the north exit. When they were finished, she lay in his arms, contemplating the bed they were in. "It's so big. I don't think it would fit in my room."

"Yes," he said, "we Japanese pay much money for space. Even in the countryside."

She stroked his hair. "What's your first name?"

"I told you. Sato."

"That's your family name?"

"Yes."

This was a common mistake. In Japanese, the last name comes first. "I mean your given name."

"Oh. Toshiyuki. You can call me Toshi."

"Do you have a girlfriend?"

Awkward silence filled the room.

"Well, do you?"

"Yes. For seven years."

"Well, I guess that I'm not really—"

"I love you." He meant it, too. "But why do you need a Japanese man? You can have a much bigger foreign man."

"You're almost a hundred and eighty centimeters tall."

More silence.

Finally Bibi clued in. "Oh, you mean, one with a bigger penis?" Her Swedish background was showing its tactlessness.

Toshi turned away from her.

"Well," she said, "you're actually a bit bigger than my current boyfriend."

He turned back to her. "Really?"

"By a little bit. But it doesn't matter. Not all white men have bigger…uh…assets…than Japanese."

He smiled. "You women are more interested in the size of a man's wallet."

Bibi rolled her eyes. But she didn't deny it.

He massaged her neck. "I had sex with my Japanese girlfriend. But I thought of you. Of your blue eyes."

Bibi smiled. She was falling for him, too. Things were looking up for life in Japan. It got better when she got a call from one of the German teachers she worked with on

Mondays. Ikea was looking to start language lessons for its management employees in Shin-Yokohama. It turned out to be enough to cover half a month's rent. For three hours on a Monday night. After the second week of class she got paid with an envelope of cash. She met Sato-san at a posh okonomiyaki restaurant. They chatted, while the chef at the teppanyaki counter fried up two of the savory pancake-like dishes. He even made a theatrical display of garnishing the okonomiyaki with mayonnaise and bonito flakes. Bibi dug in with her chopsticks. It was delicious. Especially with a glass of Yamanashi white wine.

Sato-san, or Toshi, as she now called him, was surprised when she picked up the bill for dinner. "You've won the lottery," he said.

She explained about the new class.

He looked her in the eye. "Would you like to move in with me?"

Bibi almost spat out the wine she was sipping. "We just met."

"Yeah, but I love you. It might never happen again."

"I don't know. It's so expensive. And I have a boyfriend…."

"Do you love him?"

"No, of course not."

"Then, do you love me?"

"Yes."

"So…."

"Well, are you going to break up with your girlfriend, the Japanese one?"

"Yes."

56

"And your parents won't mind?"

"It's my decision. They will be happy for me. They want me to move out, anyway. Because I work for a bank."

"Why? Does that mean you're rich?"

"Better off than most."

"But what about key money?"

"I have savings. I will pay. But I want to live in Ebisu. Near work."

"Well, it IS good for food."

"If you want me to pay for everything, I will. I can afford it. You will see. In Japan, the woman handles all the money."

"What does the man handle?"

"The beer. If his wife gives him enough money."

Bibi laughed. "Maybe. But I have a vacation booked with my current boyfriend. I can't cancel. My co-workers are going too."

"I don't disapprove. As long as you go with me the next time. Unless you want to break up."

"You don't trust me?"

PART THREE

THE

PREVIOUS FEBRUARY

10

Tuesday was Yuko's early day at work. Most of the staff came in at one in the afternoon and stayed until ten or ten-thirty at night. With one hour for lunch. She usually kept similar hours, but because the location was extra busy The Boss asked someone to come in on weekday mornings. For early classes, and in case someone stopped in looking to buy lessons. It was also a bit of a sucker's game. Most of the staff saw their bi-annual bonuses determined by the amount of sales they made. Taking the morning shift almost promised that the branch would be a ghost town.

While working mornings meant a hit to her bonus, it did allow Yuko to leave work early. Usually she went home. But tonight she got off the train in Ikebukuro, ten minutes north of Shinjuku. The opposite direction from her parents' house in Yokohama. It was unlikely she would run into someone she knew here. This was something she had done quite a few times in the past, and increasingly in the last few months.

Yuko walked to the north exit, which, although one of many in the massive station complex, was by far the seediest. The area was walled in by signs for love hotels, massage parlors, and video boxes where lonely guys rented pornography.

It was here that Yuko went to hit on men. If you had told her ten years ago that she would be seen doing this, she would have shook her head in disbelief. But now she was getting up on her thirties. And hadn't had a boyfriend in three years. She was lonely. Sex, even if it was bad, made her feel better.

The first couple of times she had been stopped by one of the yakuza who loitered around the north exit. He started asking questions. She ignored him, and kept approaching men. The yakuza who bothered her were always extremely short and ugly, dressed in tacky faux-leather coats bought on the cheap at some stall in Harajuku. By the third or forth time they stopped hassling, leaving her be, more amusement than competition. Yuko figured they might even be placing wagers on her.

She made conspicuous efforts, trying to talk to the younger men dressed in suits, then moving her targets up in age as she got more desperate. Despite coming here fifteen or twenty times in the past year, on only five occasions had she actually found someone to go to bed with her.

Yuko stood outside the Yoshinoya. This was where single men went to eat a bowl of gyuudon before heading home. As they walked by she approached, nuzzling up against them.

Between eight o'clock and ten-thirty, she did this fourteen times. She was exact in her counting. Yet none responded. Every single one ignored her. Maybe they thought she was a prostitute. Or a crazy person. Whatever it was, no one stopped.

At half past ten she descended the stairs back to the station. This was the latest she ever stayed out. After that, one of her coworkers might walk by. Tonight she felt even more depressed by her failure to attract anyone. Tomorrow she had a meeting with The Boss to discuss her inability to meet sales targets. Yuko knew she was likely to be lambasted. Rather unfair since she worked mornings twice a week. The only thing reassuring was that The Boss was mostly going through the motions. This was how the game was played. But Yuko found it stressful nonetheless.

The other thing that had set off her desire was the conversation between Dewey and Bibi the other night. How could Bibi have wanted her to kiss Dewey? Was this some sort of Swedish fetish? Despite her protestations, Yuko was kind of excited by the prospect of making out with him. He wasn't the best looking, but she was desperate. Even if Bibi wanted to watch. It was all so weird that such a thing excited her. She knew it wasn't right. Wasn't normal. But the older she got, the less she cared. She would see Dewey again on Saturday. Maybe he might approach her. But even if he didn't, she still had the vacation to spend time with him.

She got back to Yamate station in Yokohama around eleven-thirty. Stopped at the nearby liquor store and bought a bottle of umeshuu and some soda water. She enjoyed the sweet plum wine. It was not that strong when drunk straight, but she still liked to water it down. Made it easier to consume faster, letting the effects settle in. And she rarely got a bad hangover from it. Unlike beer or regular wine.

She took it home and sat in the darkened living room. She drank glass after glass until her head felt like it was swimming. Her only consolation. In a world she felt helpless to change. A wave of sadness overwhelmed her. Why had all her friends managed to get married and start families? What was wrong with her? Amid the darkness and the hum of the electric heater, she began to cry. She stayed like this, wrapping herself up in a ball, for about fifteen minutes before turning on the television. With the volume on low, she watched a show about snow crab restaurants in Tottori, polishing off the rest of the bottle.

She awoke the next day at ten. The night before, despite her drunkenness, she'd managed to collect herself. Take a shower. Walk to her room and unfurl her futon on the floor. Now, as bright sunlight streamed in, she gathered the sleeping mat up and threw it over the balcony rail before heading to the kitchen to prepare a breakfast of rice, natto, and miso soup.

The house still felt empty to her. Her father had died of stomach cancer three years ago. Only sixty-two. She wondered how life expectancy could be so long in Japan. It never seemed like any of the people she knew lived long and happy lives. Stomach cancer was pretty common. Maybe it was all the mercury in the tuna, or the stress of a corporate existence. Or even the soy sauce. But Yuko firmly believed it was the alcohol. All the bile, billowing up from the esophagus. From the stomach. That was the real cause.

Yuko had half-finished her bowl of rice when she heard the front door slam shut. Her mother, Makiko, was home from ikebana class. Her new hobby. She'd done it for six months, and would probably continue for another six before boredom set in.

"I'm home," yelled Makiko. "Can you help me with this?"

Begrudgingly Yuko got up from her breakfast. She walked out of the kitchen into the genkan to find her mother carrying the most exotic and beautifully colored arrangement of flowers she'd ever seen. "It's lovely."

"Yes. Don't you like the vase?"

It too was exotic, like a prop from a science fiction film. "I do. Is this your final project?"

"No," said Makiko, "only the mid-course assignment. We still have three more. I wish I could do one for a wedding."

The words stung. So much Yuko wanted to smash the vase on the ground. Every morning it was the same thing. A variation on 'When are you going to get married?'

Yuko's older sister Rie was already pregnant with her second child, living in Hachioji, married to a salesman for Kenwood. Yuko knew her mother saw Rie as the more successful of the two of them. If she'd known how many men Rie had test driven before she'd settled on a salesman, she wouldn't be so rude.

But Yuko said nothing. Cleared a spot on the table for the vase and resumed her breakfast.

"Yes, it is very good," said Makiko, who began to fill the rice cooker.

Yuko finished her miso soup and went upstairs to lie down. She had a slight hangover from the umeshuu. After a quick ten-minute nap, she got up and put on her work clothes. A powder blue blouse with a grey skirt and matching suit jacket. After checking her makeup, she headed down to the kitchen. Her mother had prepared her lunch. She left quickly, happy to be out of the house.

It was at Yamate station where the day began to fall apart. The Keihin-Tohouku Line was delayed. A suicide. This meant her commute in to Tokyo would be crowded and miserable. If she made it to work on time it would be a miracle.

11

Yuko waited on the train platform. It was a quarter after twelve. By now she had given up any hope of arriving at work on time and had phoned the office to let them know. She could hear the contempt in The Boss's voice. The only thing that all Japanese held sacred was that you never showed up late for work. The only possible excuse was a late train. Yuko dutifully grabbed a lateness note from the station attendant. Once at work it would be taped to a form which reported the incident and then filed away at central headquarters. Of course there was nothing she could do if someone jumped onto the tracks. But despite the blamelessness, Yuko would enter work all frazzled. Someone would have to make excuses for her. At least it wasn't summer, when the heat and humidity conspired for extra humiliation.

It was half past twelve before the trains were running again. Only local service to Yokohama station. That meant she would get to work in roughly an hour.

The train arrived. The platform wasn't crowded, but inside the train was. Yuko pushed her skinny frame through, finding a space between two men in suits.

Her body rubbed up against the man next to her. He was young. She couldn't see his face. He was right behind her as the train took off. In the right position for fucking. She wobbled back and forth. They hit a bump. Her buttocks bumped his crotch. She bumped back more, thrusting a bit rougher with each wobble.

The man turned around.

Why? she wanted to cry out. What was so wrong with her? But Yuko knew. She was too skinny. Rail thin. Flat chested. This wasn't what men wanted. If only her breasts were larger. She could smother guys like she saw in those AV films her ex-boyfriend liked to watch. Her mouth was too small, as well. She wished it were bigger. To take in more.

She changed trains in Yokohama to the Shonan-Shinjuku Line, which was running on time. The train was less crowded, so Yuko moved towards the front. It arrived closer to the south exit of Shinjuku station. She caught a glimpse of Mount Fuji as the train passed over the Ome River. Unusual. Normally it was shrouded by clouds in the afternoon. Maybe this day wouldn't be so bad after all.

Yuko had worked at the Shinjuku branch of the ABC Language Academy for five years. Still on contract. Part of her wanted the security and respect of being a full time employee. After all, contract staff were the second-class citizens of the Japanese corporate world. But being a regular employee meant the company could transfer her anywhere with only three days notice. And though she had to renew her contract annually, after you'd worked for a year they pretty much accepted that you'd stay forever, unless you quit.

She wished she could work at a branch closer to her home. There were plenty of schools in Yokohama. The fact she hadn't moved around was a bit of a black mark against her. She knew she wasn't the best employee, but she was pleasant. And reliable. So she never worried about her job security.

For a while Yuko had hoped for a promotion. For over a year she had stayed an extra hour and a half at work every night. Until last train. It was only when she heard two of the bosses talking about their universities that she clued in. Only university graduates had any hope of moving above the rank of salesperson. All the overtime in the world wouldn't change that.

Still, selling English lessons was better than her old job. Changing bedpans at the old people's daycare. In Kawasaki. Every day she had to take the Nambu Line. A train she hated. The people were trashy, the train cars old. And crowded. With weak air conditioning.

Back then she would arrive at the facility at six-thirty in the morning. Prepare for the first arrivals. Meet the wives dropping off their elderly family members before work. Some of the patients were picked up at their homes by minivan. Once Yuko had to assist on the collection route. It wasn't so bad. Except for one man with Alzheimer's. He was always trouble. She knew him well. He'd spend the day yelling for help. Desperate to know where he was. Other times he screamed like he was in a burning building. The staff had been instructed to ignore him except for regular checks. Yuko found this cruel. For the first few days. But gradually his screams of fear and desperation faded into the background. After that experience, she decided that cigarettes, alcohol, and junk food might rob you of your life, but at least they did so before time robbed you of your sanity. Then, at the end of the day, that same senile man was returned home, like a parcel sent to the wrong address. She wondered what his family felt as they tried to fall asleep against the sound of his ramblings in the background.

The train pulled into Shinjuku station. Yuko walked as fast as she could. Headed out the New South Exit to the school. Which was above a pharmacy. The first person she saw when she punched in was The Boss.

"When you have a moment, let's talk."

Yuko filled with dread.

When she walked into the classroom on the west end of the floor, she was greeted not only by The Boss, but by Nana-san. Nana was the head of the Kanto area. A woman around the age of fifty, she was married to her job, as her co-workers often said. She was one of the few that had persisted in working at ABC long after any other women might be expected.

"Come in," said Nana, gesturing to the ten empty seats in front of her. "Sit down."

"How are you? Did you come in all the way from Chiba?"

"Yes," said Nana, "we wanted to discuss your sales record."

For the next twenty minutes Nana-san went line by line with every customer Yuko had sold lessons to in the last six months. Then lectured her for ten minutes more. Yuko sat there and listened. Didn't say a word, despite wanting to burst into tears.

Later, when she returned to the main office area, Megumi saw the look on her face and followed her into the break room.

"Don't take it seriously," said Megumi. "They gave me the same lecture."

"Really?" Yuko was still fighting back tears.

"It's routine. Because you've been here so long. They don't care about your sales that much. It's considered to be out of our control. But such a speech is part of a checklist they have somewhere. Even if you were the best salesperson every year, they'd still berate you."

At that moment, a booming "Hello" filled the room.

It was Roderick, the tall handsome Australian instructor. Yuko grabbed his hand. He was surprised. "Well, aren't I a popular fellow."

"Yuko's been having a bad day."

Roderick put his arm around her, a completely bizarre thing to do to his coworker, but Yuko welcomed it. "Well, cheer up. I'm here to make you feel better."

This made Yuko smile.

12

Yuko knew Bibi had a break around seven in the evening. A half-hour between classes. In the back room Bibi found her eating lunch. A small bento box of rice and hamburger, which she was ashamed to say was made by her mother most days. She usually put off eating as long as possible, until she was absolutely starving. Eating enough food to get her through the last three hours of work.

"So," said Bibi in her usual gregarious way, "Dewey and I talked about your idea."

"What's that?"

"He wants to go camping."

Yuko looked at her blankly. "I don't really...go camping." Then the memory came rushing back. She was the one who suggested they book the campsite in the first place. Why had she said such a thing? "I only did it once. When I was a child."

Bibi unrolled a map on the counter next to Yuko. "This is the hotel we're staying at—" She pointed to a small town on the Akita coast. "But there's a mountain nearby, with a lake on the other side."

"I've heard of this part of Akita," said Yuko, putting down her chopsticks. "No one goes camping there. It is not famous."

"That's the whole point. It'll be far away. No one to bother us."

"On Golden Week it will be cold."

"We'll get some warm sleeping bags. It'll be fine."

Yuko didn't look convinced.

"Trust me, I'm Swedish. We go camping in the wintertime."

"In the snow?"

"Of course. It's actually better. Good for insulation. Bibi glanced at the map. We'll light a fire. Maybe go swimming. All the better if no one's around."

"I suppose."

Bibi pointed out a road. "We can park at the campsite. If we wanted to, we could hike all the way around the lake and up the mountain."

"I believe that is Yamanouchi Mountain."

"Yes, you can hike all the way over to the town where we're staying."

"But what about the car?"

"Yeah." Bibi thought for a moment. "That's a problem. But we can still go swimming in the lake. And everything else. Dewey says he wants to cook marshmallows over a campfire."

"Marsh…what?"

"It's some sort of thing they do in America. But it sounds like fun. And we'll save some money. We can spend an extra three days there."

Yuko rolled her eyes. "Just camping? What if it rains?"

"We can bring a tarp. That'll keep the rain away."

"Okay," said Yuko. She didn't say no, but now it would be twice as hard to find another person. But after dealing with The Boss, no part of her wanted to argue.

13

Later that week Yuko felt better. She had been trading text messages with Roderick. It was fun to have someone's attention. For the first time in a long while. Walking with a spring in her step, she wandered through the department store in the basement of Yokohama station. It was a vast complex of stores, like an underground mall. She didn't go there often. Too many old people blocking the way. But today she wanted to check out a new Swedish bakery that had opened in the basement of the Takashimaya department store.

Yuko navigated through the crowded supermarket. She rarely bought food here because it was so expensive. Indeed, it seemed difficult to spot shoppers below retirement age. Past the meat counter she saw the lineup for the Swedish bakery. It had been on TV. Now everyone in Yokohama had come down to see what the fuss was.

Yuko stood in line for the next twenty minutes. One of the bakery staff cut in front of her. Carrying a load of freshly washed trays. In Japan customers grabbed one of these trays and a pair of tongs, loading up with the baked items of their choice before proceeding to the checkout, where the clerk would bag their goodies in transparent plastic. It allowed the patrons to examine the food items for freshness before making a selection.

Yuko was about to grab a tray when her phone buzzed. It was Roderick. They had been trading texts for the past few days. He was replying to her message from yesterday. "Are you busy tonight? I'll be in Yokohama."

Yuko looked over at the tables lined with pastries and cheesecakes. Was she going to munch on sweets all alone? Or actually have a chance at getting laid?

Yuko left the lineup and texted him back. "I am busy, until eight o'clock," she wrote. A complete lie.

Roderick: "Want to go for drinks then?"

Yuko: "Where?"

Roderick: "Kannai."

Yuko: "Okay."

Promptly at eight-fifteen Yuko showed up. She'd spent the past two hours at the Yurindo bookstore, close to the Takashimaya.

Roderick was still dressed in his work wear. "How are you?"

"Good," she said. "Are you off work already?" Many instructors for the eikaiwas didn't finish work until nine-thirty.

"It's my early day. Where should we go? I don't know this area that well."

"How about yakitori?"

"Is that the one with the slices of beef? On the tabletop barbecue?"

"No, it's the chicken parts on sticks. Cooked on a hibachi."

"Sure. I could do that."

They wandered the streets until they found a place with two empty counter seats. Roderick ordered beer for them both. Then looked over the menu. "No pictures."

"No, not in yakitori. Do you want me to translate?"

"Sure."

"Well, the first one is chicken gizzard. After that is chicken skin with salt, chicken heart, chicken ears, chicken hip, and chicken thigh."

"I see."

"Then chicken liver." She pointed to the other side of the menu. "This is chicken meatball with onion. And this is chicken breast with plum sauce."

"Oh, that sounds good."

And so they spent the rest of the evening drinking beer and munching on skewers of barbecued chicken. They had been there for hours when Yuko checked the time. Quarter to twelve. "Well, it's almost time for the last train."

"One more beer," said Roderick.

"I don't know. Tomorrow I work at eleven."

"You can have one more drink."

"I don't know…." Yuko got up to go to the washroom.

Roderick smiled. "I'm ordering."

"Fine," she said, giving in. When she returned there were four mugs on the table. "It's too many."

"I think I made a mistake," said Roderick. "I thought I was ordering two, but it might have been four."

Yuko rolled her eyes. She had until one-fifteen for the last train. By the time they finished all the drinks. She had less than ten minutes to get to the station. "We've got to go."

Roderick paid the bill, a rather substantial sum. Yuko was happy.

They emerged from the yakitori-ya, onto a small side alley. "Now, where is the train station?" he said.

"I don't know," said Yuko. "I don't go to Kannai often."

They wandered the side streets, confused by their every turn. Yuko checked her cell phone. "It's one-twenty. It's too late."

"Damn, I'm sorry. We can try to find a McDonalds."

"Okay, but let me call my mother." After a brief conversation, Yuko and Roderick continued on. They turned a corner, finding themselves under a bright pink neon sign.

Roderick smiled. "What is this?"

"It is a hotel."

He examined the sign. "Let's go in."

"But that's only for when you have a girlfriend."

He took her hand. "But I'm really tired. I have to teach children tomorrow. They'll expect me to be genki."

Yuko rolled her eyes, but let him pull her in.

That night they did anything but sleep. After relaxing in the hot tub together, they fooled around on the king-sized bed. Then Yuko, for the first time in two years, got laid. And slept well. For the first time in months.

They checked out promptly at ten the next morning with everyone else in the hotel. Roderick seemed bemused that all the guests would depart at exactly the same time. But that was the way things worked in Japan.

Yuko had just enough time to get the train to Shinjuku and grab a coffee before arriving at work. As usual, the place was deserted, except for Megumi, who also worked there on Tuesday mornings. She took one look at Yuko's outfit and smiled. "Had a busy night?"

"I had a very good night." Yuko knew that now everyone in the office, at least amongst the women, would know she'd been out fooling around, arriving back at the office with the same clothes as the night before.

On Saturday night Yuko went out with Roderick again. They went to the 270 Yen izakaya near Minato Mirai.

"So," he said, once he was on his forth beer, "how do you feel about working at the ABC school?"

"It's okay. They treat me better then other places I've worked. Do you like teaching English?"

"Not sure. I think I'm going to go back to Australia in April, when my contract is up."

This hit Yuko like a ton of bricks. It shouldn't have, but it did. In the last week she'd pinned all kinds of hopes and dreams on Roderick. Only to find out this was just another fling for him. A thing of convenience. She masked her pain with an umeshuu sour. Then dutifully went back with Roderick to his guest house and made love. But it all felt empty.

It was around midnight that she was going down on him. They had been watching a porn film on his computer, the room lit with the blue glow of the monitor. She ran her tongue down the shaft of his penis, and down over his testicles.

Her tongue felt a bump.

She still felt a bit drunk, so she ignored it.

The next day Yuko saw him at work. For the most part the day went quickly. Megumi was in one of her moods, but Yuko thought nothing of it. Until she was folding pamphlets in an empty classroom. She heard voices from the other side of the door, which was slightly ajar.

"Yeah, but I'd like to improve my Japanese." It was Roderick.

"Are you taking a class?" Megumi's voice.

"No. Actually. But could you help me? You're fun to talk to."

"I don't know."

"We could go for drinks."

"I don't know...."

"Give me your LINE or you phone number, and we'll find a time...."

"Um...I'm very busy...."

Someone else interrupted Megumi in Japanese. A customer needed her help.

Yuko, however, was mortified by this conversation. So Roderick was screwing everything in sight. Well, Yuko wasn't responding to any more of his calls. She would try to get Mondays as her day off. Or work somewhere else in the Tokyo area. It could be arranged. These sorts of things had happened with foreign teachers before. The company had a process for dealing with this.

The other question was Megumi. While Yuko couldn't care less who Roderick slept with, she didn't want it to be with one of her co-workers. Part of it was jealousy, that a man would so easily cheat on her. The other was almost a feeling of protecting Megumi from such an asshole.

When Roderick was teaching one of his kids classes, they chatted in the deserted lobby.

"So," said Yuko, "what are you doing for Golden Week?"

"I don't know. My boyfriend was talking about visiting Hiroshima."

"Oh, yeah, they have the flower festival."

"But," said Megumi, "now his boss is pressuring him to go to Atami, with the other bankers on his floor. So he's been all wishy-washy about the whole idea."

"That's terrible. I'm going with Bibi and her boyfriend to an onsen in Akita."

"I wish I was doing that."

"Well, we're looking for a fourth person. To cut down on the costs. And if we can get someone else, we can rent a car. And go camping, too."

Megumi was receptive, but modest. "You really need another person?"

"I'll let Bibi talk to you about it. She'll be here in an hour."

14

For a day, things had been going exceptionally well for Yuko. Megumi had agreed to join their trip to Kita-Yamanouchi. Roderick had sent her an email, and she had felt absolutely no compunction to respond to it. It was a freeing feeling, the freedom to reject someone who had wronged her. Rather that having to stay with someone you hate.

All that freedom ended when she got home that night. Sitting in the hot bath, touching her genitals, she felt a bump. Right at the edge of her vulva. This was new. It couldn't be ignored. The next day she went to a hospital in Tsujido. It was in Fujisawa, a city to the west of Yokohama. The hospital had a shorter wait time to see a doctor. But, more importantly, Yuko was unlikely to bump into anyone she knew. Or any of her mother's friends.

After an hour reading a crummy novel on her phone, she was taken into the doctor's office. The physician was an ancient man with a receding hairline. She lay back on the table and put her feet up in the stirrups. He took one look at her vagina and nodded. "There are several treatment options, but I would recommend the cryofreeze. You're lucky. To only have one."

"You mean other people come in with more?"

He nodded.

"Okay," she said, "can we do this today?"

"Yes. Let me get the nurse."

The doctor disappeared for ten minutes. When he returned, both he and the nurse were wearing surgical masks. The nurse carried a long metal tube, like a thermos. She unscrewed the top and handed the doctor a Q-tip, which was easily twenty centimeters long. As pale smoke erupted from the canister, the doctor dipped in the cotton swab. Yuko felt a cool sensation for a moment at the edge of her vagina.

"Okay. We're done."

"That's it?"

"Yup. If the wart returns we'll do another treatment."

"Sure."

Leaving the doctor's office, Yuko felt both relieved and depressed. The treatment was easy and simple. But what if it returned? At least there was no pain. It was a small bit of comfort for an otherwise miserable day.

Yuko crossed the street and headed back towards the station. It had been a long time since she'd been here. Tsujido had exploded. A couple of years ago the area north of the Tokkaido Line was nothing but rice fields. Now it had all been filled in. By offices for a pharmaceutical company. Also a large mall, the Shonan Terrace. With ample parking.

Her stomach growled. She hadn't eaten yet today. She walked around the mall, which was mostly deserted, spare some new mothers with strollers. At the far corner she found an assortment of ramen counters and a McDonald's.

She didn't feel like noodles or hamburgers. Around the corner was a Sweets Paradise. An all-you-can-eat restaurant. Most of what was on offer was soft-serve ice cream and various cakes and sweets. The only non-dessert foods were curry rice and French fries. Yuko had often gone there with high school friends, but hadn't been back in years.

Still, she was miserable. It was too early to start boozing, so she would gorge herself.

Piling her tray high with ice cream and squares of various sorts, Yuko sat down in the middle of the mostly empty space. On Saturdays the place was probably packed with families. And young teenage girls who had finished Saturday morning school.

Yuko was halfway through her ice cream when a young man sat down a few tables away. She avoided his gaze, but then noticed he was coming closer.

"Yuko?"

She looked up. The face. Familiar. She clued in. "Yujirou?" She hadn't seen him since Coming of Age Day. Almost thirteen years previous. His hairline had receded. But it was the same guy.

"Yes," he said. "How are you? Do you live in Tsujido?"

"No, I had an appointment here for work. Are you still living in Yokohama?"

He shook his head. "I work for the pharmaceutical company. I live in their dormitory, on the other side of the station."

"Sit down, unless you're meeting someone."

"Um, no." He brought his tray over and they caught up. Yujirou was far from good looking, but Yuko wanted to talk to someone who wasn't her mother. And this was fine. Later they exchanged numbers. Began a correspondence. After two weeks of trading texts back and forth, he finally asked her out.

The next month came and went. They met up about half a dozen times or so. By the third time, he began to hold hands with her. By week five, Yuko was getting restless. They were walking near Kannai station on a Sunday afternoon when they found themselves beside the exact same love hotel where Yuko had done the deed with Roderick. Her wart problem had gone away, so she was feeling relaxed.

"I'm so tired."

"Do you want to go home and rest?" asked Yujirou.

"No, I want to spend some time with you. But I need to take a nap. Now."

"Okay," he said, pulling her towards the hotel. Together they walked in and selected a room. They had it until ten o'clock that night.

It was only when they sat down on the bed that Yujirou got all quiet.

Yuko ran the bath and started to get undressed. By the time she was down to her underwear Yujiro was in tears. "What is it?"

"It's embarrassing."

"Why?"

"I'm such a boy."

"No," she said, "you're a man. For me." She wrapped her legs around him.

He pushed her away, angry.

"What? Don't you like me?"

"But I haven't done this before."

"Done what?"

"I'm a cherry boy."

Yuko smiled. Moved in for a kiss. "Only for a few more minutes."

15

It was the forth time they made love that he showed her the bankbook. Yuko couldn't believe her eyes. Despite not yet being thirty-four years old, Yujirou was a millionaire. He'd patented a drug while he was in California, working for a company there. He and some friends had left to start their own lab, and each had profited handsomely when their small startup was bought by Pfizer.

It was something that never could have happened in Japan, he had told her. Like all Japanese university students, he had spent much of the third year of his undergraduate degree job hunting. For a safe salaryman job that he could start upon graduation. For whatever reason, he had not secured anything by the end of that school year. His job search extended into his fourth year. But by then, many potential employers were already eyeing students a year younger than him. He looked like damaged merchandise, left on the shelf after the store had shut its doors.

Yujirou had begged his parents for the money to do a master's degree. Of course he knew it was a signal to all employers that he couldn't hack it in the workforce. Graduate degrees are looked at with suspicion in corporate Japan. Still, he kept up learning English, and applied for a doctorate at the University of California. The day he was accepted, no one was more shocked than he.

Now, after a whirlwind five years in America, making a fortune when most of the country struggled, he had accepted a consulting position at the Japanese drug company in Fujisawa. Many of those classmates who had mocked his situation before now had to report to him, a fact they resented. The only employees with perks similar to Yujirou's were almost twice his age.

"But why are you showing me this?"

"Because I'm tired," he said, "of being alone."

"What do you mean?"

"I want to marry you."

Yuko didn't know what to say. She needed time to think. There was no way she could go through with this. They barely knew each other. And he'd never had another girl. What if he got tired of her? Or if he couldn't handle living with another person?

She took his hand and gazed into his eyes.

"Well," he said, "will you?"

Yuko closed her eyes. "Okay."

Her mother was ecstatic when she heard the news. So were

all her friends. Later that week Yujirou phoned her. "Where do you think we should live? How about Kamakura."

"It's nice. But I like Yokohama."

"I know, but it's awful close to my parents. Do you really need to live there?"

"I suppose not. But I like to go shopping there."

When she put down the phone, Yuko saw she had another message from Roderick. As usual, it went right into the trash.

So it was a surprise, the next morning, in an empty school, that Roderick showed up.

Megumi was manning the front desk. "What are you doing here? I thought you moved to the Chiba branch."

"I was forced to go. I have no idea why. In the middle of the year. It takes me almost an hour and a half to get to work now. Did you know that?" He scowled. "Is she here?"

"Who?"

"Her."

"Who?"

"Yuko."

"Let me check."

Yuko was indeed there. Hiding in the back room. She shook her head, making the 'shhh' signal. No way she wanted to talk to Roderick.

Megumi came back out. "I'm sorry, but she has been transferred."

"Huh? You just talked to her. She's right back there. I can see her reflection in the mirror."

Megumi looked back. It was true. "She doesn't want to talk to you. Go away."

"I want to speak to her."

"No. Go." She was already on the phone with headquarters.

"I'm not leaving until she comes out."

"Fine. Go sit down."

Roderick sat for a few minutes, but then must have clued in to what would happen, and took off before the supervisor from headquarters arrived.

Later that night, over yakitori, Yuko related the exact story to Yujirou. Except that Megumi, not her, had occupied the role of Roderick's affections in Yuko's version of the story.

"Yes," said Yujirou, "foreigners can be crazy. Some of them do strange things because they are in a foreign country. If it were America, he would have brought a gun."

"That's terrible." She took his hand. "My mother asks me every day, 'When are you going to get married?'"

Yujirou smiled. "I like September"

PART
FOUR
THE
PREVIOUS
MARCH

16

She was a stunner and she knew it.

Megumi first became aware of it at the start of junior high school. She got just a little more attention than the other girls. Getting laid, should she want to, was never a problem. Of course, her high school had been tiny. Miyazaki wasn't exactly the largest prefecture in Japan. It was hard to get to, not being on a bullet train route. Her hometown was called Kushima, always a difficult place to explain since the Fukushima meltdown. People heard where she was from and asked if her family had been evacuated. Then she would have to tell them she was from Kyushu, on the other side of Japan. No nuclear reactors there.

She liked living in Kanto, even if people here in the Tokyo area were a bit cold. They always seemed unwilling to get to know people, and they loved giving bullshit excuses for everything.

From her purse Megumi took out a compact mirror and checked her lipstick. Her mouth was full and sensuous, the kind that attracted attention. Her eyes were big, more like a white girl than an Asian. Her breasts were full, but not fat, coupled with a slender waist. She wished she was taller, like some of the foreign girls. A lack of stature was a common problem in the Japanese countryside, where a traditional diet low in beef and milk products was common. Miyazaki was famous for its cows, so that was less of a problem than, say, Wakayama or Gunma. And most of all, her teeth were perfect. Perhaps too perfect. Megumi thought the little fangs that many Japanese girls had were cute, and wished she'd had that particular flaw herself. She'd even gone so far as to explore the price of getting dental treatment to adjust her teeth. But the effort and cost didn't seem worth it.

Putting away the compact she lit a cigarette. The second floor of the Café Excelsior in Roppongi was crowded this afternoon. The table in front of her was covered with paperwork. Budgets. Sales targets. Memos. She had worked for the ABC Company for so long that this was becoming her life. Management.

It hadn't always been this way. Just out of high school she'd been accepted to a fashion college in Vancouver. Sure, her English was terrible. And the job market could be difficult. Still, she dreamed of working in New York or Paris. But her parents were dead set against it. Too far from home. She also got accepted to the Tokyo University of Agriculture. At her mother's insistence, she studied landscape architecture.

It certainly had its creative aspects, like designing gardens and figuring out what plants grew in which climates. But she didn't feel the passion for it, and she didn't like working outside. While many of her classmates had chosen to work in related fields, she'd gone straight into working for an eikaiwa. An ABC school in Kyoto.

After a couple of years, she'd been transferred back to Tokyo. She started going out again with her old boyfriend, who worked for a bank. And life continued on. Boring, but comfortable. She had an apartment in Shimo-Kitazawa, a trendy-enough part of Tokyo.

Today she was meeting her comfortable-enough boyfriend after he met with clients in Roppongi. This was the section of Tokyo with the highest concentration of foreign embassies, and where the Ritz-Carleton Hotel was located. It was also where many prominent celebrities kept apartments, in the tall buildings that towered over the expressways and the Nigerian hostess club hustlers.

A man and a woman sat down next to her. The man was dressed in a suit, like every other salaryman. With her headphones on, Megumi couldn't hear their conversation. She pressed pause for a second. The man was trying to convince the woman to work at a hostess bar. Then there was talk about films.

The woman must be an adult film actress. There was no other way. Not with the way they were talking. The man mentioned an address in Azubu-Juban. Then talked to the girl about the future. Her career prospects were dim. The agent must be trying to squeeze the last bits of revenue out of her. Megumi knew this because she, as a college student, had worked at a hostess bar in the same building. It always came as a surprise to her when foreigners talked about what was known in Japan as the "water trade." So named after all the women who drank-watered down drinks to remain sober while the men who paid to chat with them drank themselves under the table.

Still, it was good money for the girls. The only downside was the stalkers. Always the men wanted to see her outside of the club, after hours. Of course, if one of the girls were to do this, the guy would have no incentive to come back. The mama-san—the older woman who managed the place—would lose income. So outside entanglements were a strict no-no.

Of course, many of the female teachers who came to Japan thought this system was sexist and lecherous. Until Megumi explained how much you could make, just drinking EXTREMLY weak cocktails and putting up with old men's bullshit. In fact, it was pretty much the same as being an English teacher in Japan, except for the alcohol part. And the part about making lots of money.

Those days came to an end when her boyfriend at the time, the manager of the bar, asked her to do a porno film. 'No' was the first word out of her mouth. She hadn't come all the way from Miyazaki to do that kind of work. Then he suggested she could do delivery health, which entailed going to love hotels and giving blowjobs. Also a no. Shortly after that he became aggressive. Once he tried to slap her, but he was so skinny that when she punched back, he doubled over in surprise as much as in pain. After that he had tried to make up excuses that porn could be a stepping-stone to a legitimate career. She laughed, demanded to be paid out from the mama-san, and never returned. Then started dating the banker.

Megumi felt almost bad for the girl next to her. Almost. Anyone who is paid to have sex in front of a camera knows what they're getting into, as far as she was concerned. Still, it wasn't all that far removed from the rest of the Japanese entertainment industry. Think of all those girls in AKB48. That was the all-girl group who had been formed as a gimmick to promote electronics in Akihabara. Forty-eight girls. Enough band members that they could rotate the cast for performances. Their main audience seemed to be the fat, smelly otaku crowd. Clamoring to see the group's daily live shows. Each of the girls had been recruited to look pretty much the same. Once they got close to legal age they "graduated" to obscurity. Although recently more and more were "graduating" to porn. Not to mention those poor girls who'd been knifed by a deranged fan at an autograph session in Aomori a few months back. The whole thing stank, she thought. Agents and promoters taking advantage of naïve young girls who knew nothing about the entertainment industry. Which Megumi was convinced was controlled mostly by the yakuza. Or at least the domestically based media companies were.

She leaned back and lit up a cigarette. Of course, working the counter at a language school was often like working at a hostess club. On Sundays there were two male students in particular, both in their early-20's, who had a tendency to hang around long after their lessons. Just to talk to the female Japanese staff. It had never been a problem, not like the one which Yuko had brought in with Roderick. But it was still annoying. Half her day was chatting to lonely young men, the other half convincing parents that spending money on English lessons once a week really made a difference in their children's future.

Her phone vibrated. It was The Boyfriend.

"Can you come meet me in Iidabashi?"

Megumi sighed. Her relationship was beginning to feel like a chore.

17

It was a nightmare changing at Hibiya station this time of day. She rarely took the Yurakucho Line, but it was the cheapest route. After getting lost for ten minutes, Megumi finally found the right platform.

Iidabashi was in the center of Tokyo. It seems The Boyfriend's meeting schedule had changed. Megumi rarely came here, because the center of the Metropolis, while filled with organizations and corporate headquarters, had a scarcity of women's clothing stores. Why couldn't they have met in Shinjuku? It was on the way home for both of them. Of course, there was The Theory.

Megumi was convinced that The Boyfriend was cheating on her with an OL. According to The Theory, the OL lived somewhere east. Probably near Shin-Koiwa. For those of you not accustomed to Japanese office politics, OL stands for office lady. It is the lowest of all positions in the white-collar hierarchy, reserved for young women. Tasks mainly involve filing paperwork and making tea for the men who sit at the top of the management structure. Most OLs retire from the company when they get married, these days anywhere from their late-twenties to early thirties.

It was a job Megumi couldn't fucking imagine doing.

Especially for one of those old-school Japanese companies.

Recently she'd began to suspect The Theory because The Boyfriend had seemed especially distant from her. Of course, he was from Saitama, so that wasn't a surprise. He was cute and well dressed, so that kept her from dumping him outright. And he did work for a bank. What more secure job could you ask for? Better than those dolts who worked at the language academy. In her way, she might even love him. Maybe. It was more an arrangement of convenience. For both of them.

He was waiting for her outside of the Beckers. She nodded at him. "How was your day?"

"Not over yet. I still have to go back to the office."

"So that's why you met me here?"

"Yes."

They went upstairs to the burger restaurant. Megumi ordered the mentaiko fries. The boyfriend got a burger and a coffee. "So, how are the foreigners at work?"

"Crazy." She told him the story of Yuko's Australian boyfriend. "She should have known better. There were plenty of rumors of how possessive he is. But she's so stupid. No brains at all. I have to recheck her paperwork all the time. That's why we put her on the morning shift." Megumi picked at her French fries. "There is one thing that the foreign men do for their girlfriends, though."

"What's that?"

"They always celebrate the anniversary of their first date."

"Every year?"

"Yes. You remember ours was…."

"On a tennis club trip. Over Golden Week."

"Yes." This was followed by an uncomfortable pause.

"But," he said, "the boss wants us to go on a company retreat to Hakone."

"They asked you?"

"No, but I'll know soon."

"Well, if that's the case, I've been invited by Yuko and some coworkers to an onsen."

"You said she was stupid."

"But I still like spending time with her."

"Go. I have to work during most of your holidays anyway. I should start an eikaiwa. Just for the vacation."

"You wouldn't like the pay. Speaking of which, my lease is up at the end of May. I have to start saving for the key money soon." Megumi had an apartment in Musashi-Kosugi. It was a major station in the center of Kawasaki that connected the Tokyu Lines with the Shonan-Shinjuku and Yokosuka Line. Her apartment wasn't large, but it was in a new building with plenty of security. An important feature if you're a pretty girl in Tokyo. The only problem was that to get such a nice apartment—less than three minutes from the Toyoko Line station—she had to pay the equivalent of four months rent in key money. Her lease was for a standard two years, but when it came up for renewal, she'd have to pay the key money again.

"Yes," said The Boyfriend.

"We've been together for eight years. Don't you think it's time?"

"Well, I need to think. Why don't you renew your lease? When I'm ready, I could move in there."

"It's an all-female building. The landlord would give me a hard time. Besides, I'm tired of paying excessive rent. With two incomes we could rent a much nicer place."

"Living with my parents saves a lot of money."

Megumi didn't know what to say to that. She had made it clear that there was no way she was moving in with his family. She hated Saitama, and had no intention of becoming a nurse for grumpy old people. He still had a younger sister at home. She could take care of the parents when the time came.

They resumed eating in silence. After he finished his coffee they departed, making plans to meet up on Sunday. Megumi took the JR line back to Shinjuku, changing trains there. She was angry at the way he was treating her. Like a temporary mistress. Eight years. A long time for both of them. If they weren't married soon, what could she be looking forward to? At least he wasn't a total drunk, like most men his age. But he certainly wasn't creative. He was just…secure. Boring.

That summed up her life. Secure. But boring. More than anything, she wanted some excitement.

18

First, there is the issue of your sales," said The Boss. "As you know, the economy right now is doing well. But the figures for this location have not improved in the last two years. We need to do something about this. We're looking at bringing in new people."

Megumi was aghast. The moment she'd arrived at work, the old hag had dragged her into the back room. Presented her with a bunch of reports. This was awful.

"Then there are the issues, here, and—" The Boss handed her another piece of paper— "here. We've had headquarters correct all your mistakes on the paperwork. But this is a pattern. We've held a meeting about it, and it has been the decision to move you to a position where you can focus more on your sales skills."

"What?" said Megumi, barely able to speak.

"You will become the sales representative for intensive classes at the Yokohama branch."

Megumi wanted to punch the woman in the face. She'd been with the company since university. Ninety-five percent of the people who worked here had failed or quit another job before getting hired at the ABC Language Academy. Which meant they were the rejects of the Japanese corporate world. Everybody who took a job at the age of twenty-two held on to it at all costs, unless it was so unbelievably shitty that no one wanted it. There were only three or four people on the entire Kanto staff who had been hired at university graduation. Megumi was one of them. Now it was time for revenge. By the people who had failed in life. The Boss, one of them. Unmarried, and unable to push through the glass ceiling, she was coming after Megumi.

"Of course," said The Boss, "since these new duties carry a heavy workload, we will be giving you a raise. And you'll be eligible for additional bonuses."

Maybe this wouldn't be so bad, she thought. "Who is the head of the branch there?"

"XX. You know him from Osaka, right?"

Megumi went cold. XX was a serial rapist.

She had first encountered him when she worked in Kyoto. After graduating from Nodai, the ABC Company had hired her, but they only had a position available in Kansai, the area where Osaka, Kyoto, and Kobe are located. With few other prospects, Megumi took the job. She landed in a tiny school in Shiga, the prefecture next to Kyoto. Even then, she had heard stories about XX. A fifty-year old manager that worked in Osaka.

Again, they were just rumors. Of the man keeping an apartment near the school. Luring the staff back under the auspices to pick up documents, or some other excuse. Never any of the foreign teachers—XX knew that the Japanese girls were less likely to report anything. He usually chose small skinny girls. Twigs. Not like her. After three years in Shiga, Megumi had been scheduled to work with him. He was to be her new boss.

One time, just before he transferred to the Shiga school and assumed his new duties, he had taken over a shift for one of her coworkers. Came in to see the lay of the land, as it were. As is the custom in Japan, no one goes home until the boss leaves. Since XX was the boss, she didn't leave until he was ready. Which was well after her usual shift. They were all alone when he locked the front door. Then forced himself on her. She had swatted him away easily, bitched him out, then left, threatening to report it to the police if he did anything. He hadn't expected such a response, but Megumi was from Miyazaki, where girls are used to putting up with such bullshit. And know how to deal with it. But in truth, she did worry about being fired. Whatever. It was better than being raped but a scrawny, wrinkly old man.

It was the next day that the shit hit the fan.

One of the students at the ABC Academy, a fourteen-year-old girl, was found at home by her father. With her English teacher inside of her. The guy was too cheap to take the girl to a hotel, so he had fucked her in her living room when one of her parents came back home unexpectedly. Calls were made to the school. The teacher was fired. And XX had a lot of explaining to do. He was the boss of the school where the fourteen-year-old took lessons. At some station in Osaka that Megumi couldn't recall. Bad timing on XX's part. It was his next-to-last week working at that particular location.

Megumi never saw him again. The next week she was transferred to the Kanto area, the region around the capital that contains Tokyo and Yokohama. Plenty of staff were often moved up from Osaka. There was a general feeling at the ABC Academy that Tokyo people didn't know how to do sales properly. Osaka had the headquarters of several chain English schools, most notoriously Nova, which had gone bankrupt. People in Osaka are generally seen as gregarious, a reminder of the city's historic merchant culture. The opposite of the cold bureaucratic drones that populated Tokyo. Truth to be told, Megumi preferred Kansai, especially Kobe. But the economy there wasn't as good. Much of Japan was hollowing out, its young workers relocating to Kanto.

But how to deal with XX? Megumi left the meeting shaking her head. Maybe it was time for her to spend that year abroad she'd always wanted to. The Yokohama branch was big, with twenty other Japanese staff. But Megumi was probably the best looking. This meant she'd inevitably have to go to drinks with XX, even if it was in a group.

It might be time to carry mace, as one of the American teachers had suggested.

19

Megumi had one strange habit that you would never expect a squeaky-voiced Japanese girl like her to have. She liked Scotch. Perhaps the only person under age fifty to do so. It was a habit she had inherited from her father. From which he, as sire to the family's company, had inherited from Megumi's grandfather. Their business was cold storage refrigeration. To Megumi it was the most boring thing on earth. But from humble beginnings it had boomed in the eighties, as demand increased overseas for sushi. This allowed her father to amass quite the collection of rare whiskeys, many bottled before she was born.

The weekend after her Coming of Age Day, Megumi's father began training her palette. So when she walked into most liquor stores she cringed at the barely-drinkable swill that most people consumed. Even in Tokyo, it was difficult to find a decent liquor store. There was one place under Tokyo station that offered thimble-sized samples of rare Scotches that were decent. But on her eikaiwa salary, buying a bottle was out of the question.

The discovery of the Scotch bar just happened one day, when Megumi was out shopping after an early day at work. She had been wandering through the narrow maze of shopping streets to the east of Shinjuku station. Stepping out of the Isetan department store, she turned a corner and spotted a sign for a basement whiskey bar. Assuming it had the normal drab selection, she planned to walk past. But at the bottom of the sign she saw a badly photocopied label for Strathisla '57. It was the end of the day, so it couldn't hurt to indulge, she thought to herself. And the salaryman crowd probably wouldn't pile in until nine o'clock. She walked down the stairs to a small narrow room, adorned with expensive leathers and woods.

A completely empty room, at that. The bow-tied barman doted on her, surprised a woman would have such sophisticated tastes in alcohol. At one point he became a bit too...endearing. Megumi, in the politest possible terms, asked him to back the fuck off. Since then she'd been left alone to sip her whiskey at the bar, on the three or four occasions per year she patronized the establishment.

Like tonight.

It really was a bizarre place, smack dab in the middle of Kabukicho. That was the name of this area of Shinjuku, the largest red light district in the country. Considered by many people to be the most dangerous part of Japan. That, however, was mostly hyperbole. It did have a lot of love hotels and hostess bars, among the bevy of other services available. Then there were the touts that occupied every corner and inter-section, trying to get male customers into their establishments. There were the yakuza types, scrawny short young men in black leather jackets that seemed to permanently occupy the streets, for reasons that Megumi didn't understand. This was their neighborhood.

A loud cacophony came from the entrance. A dozen or so aging salarymen piled into the bar. This crowd would get drunk and never leave her alone. She asked for her bill and downed the rest of her scotch and soda.

It was not until she got back up to the street that Megumi realized she was out of cigarettes. In her mild drunken haze she had forgotten that she'd left the empty pack at the bar. Stumbling in the direction towards the station, she caught sight of a Daily Yamazaki convenience store.

There was a lineup at the register. Megumi checked the train schedule on her phone. She was going to miss the Shonan-Shinjuku Line train. The next one going her way wasn't for another twenty-five minutes. She could've taken the Yamanote Line and transferred, but in her drunken state this felt like too much effort. She would wait it out. The man in front of her departed. She asked the clerk for Marlborough menthol lights.

To kill time she moved to the magazine rack. Opened up a copy of CanCam. To an article about eyeliner.

Then she saw them.

It was just a flash. Out of the corner of her eye, right above the magazine. There was no doubt that a woman with blond hair would stand out anywhere in Japan. Almost unconsciously Megumi's glance had followed the couple. It was only when the man turned his head she realized what she was seeing.

The Boyfriend.

Holding hands.

With another woman.

Megumi stood in shock. Who would do this to her? Why? How long had she been duped?

She put down the magazine and walked out. They were half a block ahead of her. Stopped at the crosswalk at Shinjuku Dori.

It wasn't difficult to maintain a discreet distance at the intersection. People were crowded in like sardines waiting for the light. There must have been hundreds of people on both sides of the road. People drunk, people happy and drunk, and people really happy, in the way that comes after a decent full frontal fucking.

The light changed. The traffic stopped and the crowd surged forward. People walking purposefully to catch the train home. She followed them across the taxi circle and into the station. Down at the ticket gate they stopped as the blond woman, a foreigner, judging by the size of her ass, was looking for her Suica card.

Megumi held back, standing behind a group of girls waiting under the electronic train schedules. She got a glimpse of the foreign woman's face, and almost ran away.

Bibi.

The Swedish teacher.

Was fucking her boyfriend.

What other reason would they be in Kabukicho for?

Fighting back tears, Megumi followed them through the gate. All the way to the Yamanote Line platform. Megumi climbed the stairs and took up a spot far away, disappearing into the crowds. The platform was almost packed to capacity. It wasn't hard to see Bibi, so blond…and taller than most everyone else.

There was a rush of wind and the train flew past. Both sides of the platform emptied out at the same time, as the Sobu Line express arrived on the other side from the Yamanote train. The two crowds intermingled. Toshi kissed the blond girl on the lips and a bit more of Megumi crumbled. Look at him—showing off his affection in public. He got on board the train, Bibi disappeared down the stairs. At least they weren't going home together.

Megumi kept an eye on him. Almost hoping he'd see her. Wanted to hear the excuse he would give.

At Ikebukuro she followed Toshi down a set of stairs and up another to transfer to the Saikyo Line. Why hadn't he just taken it from Shinjuku? Because he wasn't thinking straight, obviously. She tried to get close to him. Talk to him. Burst his bubble of bliss. But the train arrived. A wall of passengers exited, preventing her from getting any closer.

Onward they went to Musashi-Uruwa station. She had closed her eyes. The alcohol was making her sleepy. It would be a long ride back home. She got off the train at the last minute. Toshi was already at the other side of the platform. She lost sight of him until she exited the gate. Spotted him walking to get his bike.

There was only one exit for the bicycle garage. Megumi

stood right in front of it. She waited there for a couple of minutes. Toshi didn't come out. Was there a back exit?

She was about to go back and catch the train home when he appeared. His glance was downward. Slowly he peddled his bike past her, as if she was a lamppost. Megumi was shocked. She hurried after him, as fast as she could in heels. He peddled so slowly it wasn't too hard to catch up. Reaching forward she gripped his suit jacket. In shock he fell sideways crashing into the ground. Stunned, he tried to get up.

Megumi towered over him, pressing her heel into the side of his abdomen. Toshi screamed. Looked up. "Megumi?"

20

"What are you doing here?"

"You mean, you didn't see me?"

Toshi rolled around on the pavement before getting up. Pulled the bike with him. "You never come to Musashi-Uruwa."

"How about you explain what you were doing with that blond Swedish bitch?"

"I don't know what you're talking about."

"The girl on the train."

"I haven't been with anyone. I just came from work in Ebisu."

She shook her head. "Do you really think I'm that stupid? I followed you into Shinjuku station."

"This is all a misunderstanding."

"Is it? I saw you holding hands and kissing her."

Toshi took out his cell phone. It was a way of avoiding her gaze. "Maybe YOU were there cheating on me. Why else would you be in Kabukicho?"

"Think hard. Back to our last anniversary."

"We went to a hotel."

"Before that."

"We had drinks, in a basement bar."

A grin spread across Megumi's face. "That's were I was. By myself. Trying to recover from a terrible day at work. Made worse that you picked someone I work with to cheat on me. You couldn't just let it be a random chick."

His face changed. Anger appeared. "All the times I looked the other way."

"What?"

"You know exactly what I'm talking about."

"No, I don't."

"The only reason you would work for an English school is to meet foreigners." His gaze narrowed. "I know you always cheated on me with those foreign teachers. Why else would you have taken such a job?"

"That is what this is about? Some sort of imagined revenge? I've never cheated on you. Ever. I could have. But I never did. Not once." Megumi began to think. This couldn't be an isolated incident. "How many other women have you been with while you called me your girlfriend?"

Toshi didn't answer. Just kept flicking through his cell phone screen.

She slapped him. "Tell me!"

Megumi stepped back. He wasn't going to answer. It was like she was staring at her brother. The only thing she felt

118

for him was a sense of irritation. Like she was dealing with a little child. There was no point in continuing this. It was just lies and evasions. Megumi could have put up with that, but she knew this was different. He would have asked Bibi where she worked. What schools. He would have known he'd probably be caught. This was just his way of sending a signal when he didn't have the balls to tell her how he really felt. She turned around and started back to the station.

He dropped the bike and ran up the stairs behind her. "You've got to stop acting this way. I'll end it. Is that what you want?"

Megumi didn't respond. She passed through the station, leaving him behind at the gate.

21

At the end of the week, Megumi brought her concerns to The Boss. "I don't think we can afford the Swedish instructor next year."

"Really? Why's that?"

It was the monthly budget meeting. Megumi was being transferred to the Yokohama branch in a matter of weeks. She was determined that she would end Bibi's career at the ABC Language Academy. "The cost of her commutes. And we have to pay her for three hours, but we haven't been able to fill up her schedule."

The rest of the staff were shocked. No one ever talked in meetings. Usually it was just The Boss reporting figures. If anyone disagreed with them, they would chat informally, over a coffee break, or go for drinks after work. Sure, they thought, it must have to do with the fact Megumi was from southern Kyushu. To many of the other staff, particularly those from Kanto and Tohouku, it was an exotic far away place very few of them had ever been. Perhaps it was normal for women or employees to be outspoken there. But it wasn't the norm in Tokyo. Not that it was unacceptable, it was just a strange thing to do in a meeting. Of course, if such protestations became common, there was always the option of transferring Megumi back to Osaka.

"Well," said The Boss, equally surprised, "we are the largest language school chain in Tokyo. It may be expensive to keep Bibi-sensei, but we can offer German and Swedish, which is important."

Megumi became quiet after that.

In the elevator the next week, she showed The Boss a sheet she'd prepared. It was from a woman named Takahara who was taking a Swedish class from Bibi on Wednesday nights. One night the woman had come out to chat in the lobby after her lesson. She had mentioned how difficult Swedish grammar is. Megumi decided, although it was months since that conversation, to write up a complaint form. In many parts of Japan, students are reluctant to complain in a very direct way. Megumi considered the woman's comments open to interpretation.

The Boss took the form and looked it over. "Yes, it seems the student was very clear in her criticisms. But Bibi is the only teacher we can get for that night. What options do we have?"

Megumi stayed silent.

"I see," said The Boss. "Well, I have to go to headquarters for a meeting. I'll ask about getting another teacher."

That would be the last Megumi ever heard of the complaint.

Another week after that, The Boss and Megumi were chatting. The Boss was filling in for Yuko on an early Monday morning. Once again the topic had drifted to Bibi.

"Of course," said Megumi, "we'd save a lot of money if we put all the Swedish classes at one school. Maybe we could get them to take their lessons at the Iidabashi branch. That would free up resources here for more children's classes. Or a junior high school class."

The Boss nodded and thanked her for the suggestion. Later that day she approached Yuko. "Can you take them out for drinks together?"

More than a week had passed since Megumi's previous attempt to oust Bibi.

"Why?"

"I think it would be beneficial for them to get to know each other. But don't tell them in advance that each other will be there."

Yuko smiled. "Why? Is there a problem?"

"No. But it might be a good idea if they had more sympathy for each other's work. Let them get to know what kind of problems they have. Maybe they can find common ground. Together."

So Yuko set it up. That Saturday they went to the Hub on the north side of Shinjuku dori in Kabukicho. Although she rarely frequented the chain of Irish pubs that many foreigners went to, she felt it would make Bibi more at ease.

For Megumi, it was the exact opposite. What had Yuko been thinking, asking her to go out for drinks without saying

Bibi would be coming? It was clearly a set up. Everyone saw she had a vendetta, and they wanted it to end. Was she really that transparent?

Then there was the location Yuko had chosen. Practically next door to the scene of the crime. She wondered if Bibi could even find the love hotel on her own, or did she have to hold Toshi's hand to get there? But gradually as the conversation progressed to talk of boyfriends, Megumi realized that Bibi had no idea she was Toshi's girlfriend.

"Have you ever been with a Japanese guy?" asked Yuko.

Bibi smiled. "Maybe."

"But they are so much smaller than western men."

"Some. But not all." She grabbed a French fry from a measly plate of fish and chips they'd ordered. "And even in Sweden, men come in different shapes and sizes. I like men with dark hair."

"Because you are blond," said Megumi. "They like you, too."

"Yeah, well," said Bibi, "I guess I was born lucky. But not all women in Sweden are blond. Most have dark hair, just like Japan."

They kept chatting and having a good time. Megumi thought she was exceptionally well behaved. She should have gone into acting. It was on her fifth oolong tea shochu cocktail that she made the decision. All this time she had been trying to get Bibi out of her way. She should instead be holding her closer.

"So," said Megumi, "I hear you two are going to Tohouku for Golden Week."

"Yes," said Yuko, "it's going to be exciting."

"I've never been there before," said Bibi.

"Me neither," said Megumi. "I've always wanted to visit the northern onsens. Yuko said you were looking for a fourth person."

And with that, the deal was sealed. Megumi was going on vacation with them. To drop the bombshell on Dewey. About the state of affairs with Bibi. Right in the middle of the trip. Maybe at the onsen. Or some night when they were at the camp ground.

It was as simple as that. Megumi wanted them to be completely miserable. It was only a little bit of revenge, but it would suffice.

PART
FIVE
THREE
WEEKS
AGO

22

He should have been fired years ago."

"So why wasn't he?"

"The rumor is," said Yuko, "he is a relative of the owner."

Yuko and Megumi sat in the lobby of the ABC Shinjuku school. It was one of the lulls in the day, typical of the early afternoon when children's classes were in session.

"So why don't they transfer him to headquarters? Where he can't do any damage?"

Yuko looked down at her notepad. "I don't know. Someone told me he's the owner's 'eyes and ears.' Yokohama school was having difficulty with staffing. So they sent him down from Nagoya to run it."

Megumi tapped a pencil against her lower lip. "Nagoya? He was working in Osaka when I met him."

"Well, he's transferred every year or so. He's worked in almost every city in Japan. But," said Yuko, lowering her voice, "I heard that the owner doesn't even want this company anymore. He feels obligated since he was the only son. But he'd rather do something else. He wants to sell it to the Mitsubishi bank conglomerate, but they won't even consider it unless it can be made profitable. Which is almost impossible, between the state of the economy and the oversaturation of language schools."

"Of course."

"So XX has been going around, looking for places to cut costs. Load up the staff with work. Switch to more part time staff."

A group of five-year-olds burst into the lobby. All of them excited by the Easter egg crafts they'd made. Part of the English language class experience is celebrating holidays that are completely unknown in Japan. Dewey followed with a group of mothers.

"Everyone loves the Easter bunny," he said. He smiled at one of the children, and walked over to the desk. "Are you two gossiping about me?"

"Of course," said Yuko.

"I got your email about the campsite and the rental car. How are we going to pay for it?"

"I have a credit card," said Megumi.

"Yes," said Yuko, "and Bibi and I both have driver's licenses."

"Lucky you," said Dewey. As an American, he was from pretty much the only developed country where you couldn't exchange your local license for a Japanese one. Every other person he knew from Canada and Britain had gone to the department of motor vehicles, paid seven thousand yen, taken a five-second eye test, and had been issued a license. For Americans, and Chinese, it was a different matter.

As Yuko departed to chat the with the children's mothers, Megumi gazed back into Dewey's eyes. "It is complicated planning a vacation for so many people."

"Yeah. I've always stayed at hostels in the past."

"This is your first time at an onsen?"

"Yup."

"What do you call them in English?"

"Hot springs. But we don't have very many in the U.S., and never with hotels."

Megumi looked into his eyes. "Do men in America cheat on their girlfriends?"

A grin spread across Dewey's face. That was an abrupt transition, he thought. He'd never been asked such a question before. "America is a big country. People are kind of different in different places."

"And what about in California?"

"Well, I'm from Lompoc, and I went to university in Santa Cruz, so I can't speak for the rest of the state, but yeah, it's pretty liberal. Compared to say, Mississippi. But then Orange County, just outside of Los Angeles is very conservative. Lots of white supremacists. And yuppies driving 3-series BMWs."

"I see."

Dewey checked the time. He still had five minutes before his next lesson. This one with adults. "So, I've decided to take a few days off before the Golden Week holidays."

"Really?"

"Yeah. I'm going to buy one of those tickets…."

"Seishin jyuhachi kippu?"

"Yeah, that's it. Maybe I'll do some traveling before heading up to Akita. We haven't booked the campsite until the Wednesday of the week, so maybe I'll hang around town."

"There isn't much to do in the countryside."

"I'll find something to occupy my time. What do you know about Akita, anyway?"

Megumi thought about his question. "Well, I've never been there. Not to Kita-Yamanouchi. But my father worked there for a year, in Sakata. They have their own dialect."

"Like a different accent? The same as Britain and America?"

"Not exactly. They have their own words for many things. I can't understand them when they are talking in Akita-ben. It is the same in Kagoshima and Okinawa. The locals can tell if you're not one of them. My father went to go drinking and they would ignore him. They called him the 'man from headquarters' even though he was from Kyushu."

"You didn't go with him?"

"No. Many salarymen are transferred by their companies to different places. They leave their wives and children at home. But he would visit every month."

"I see. So that's why there's a national holiday every month in Japan."

"But Kita-Yamanouchi is inaka."

"You mean the country?"

"Yeah, it is terrible."

"Why?" asked Dewey. "By definition, all of America is inaka, except Manhattan."

"But Akita is worse."

"How? They have such cute dogs."

Megumi smiled at that thought. "They are cute, but people there are all descendants of samurai who lost in Western Japan."

"Huh?"

"They lost their land in Kansai, and went to Tohouku. To escape."

"I see."

"And many families are kinshin-kon."

"What?"

"When you marry your family. Like Prime Minister Kan, during the Fukushima meltdown."

"You mean, inbred?"

"Yes."

"I see. Lovely place."

"Are you excited to go on vacation with Bibi? We won't be intruding?"

"No, that's fine. It will give her someone to talk to."

"Why? You don't like to talk to each other?"

"I just feel like our relationship is drifting," said Dewey.

"Maybe you should get a new girlfriend." Megumi looked down at the paperwork she was filling out. "But be careful, many girls might cheat on you."

"Like Japanese girls?"

"Maybe."

Dewey shook his head. "I'd hate to see Bibi with another man. She's the best-looking girl I've ever dated. I don't know what I'd do."

Megumi twirled a lock of hair. "I've seen her. Waiting for you."

"Really?"

"Yeah. Outside of Kawasaki station."

"Huh?"

"At the east exit. At the bottom of the steps."

"I never meet her there. Maybe at Shibuya."

Megumi stayed quiet.

Yuko retuned to the desk. "Dewey, it is time for your next lesson."

"Sure," he said, not pressing Megumi on the issue. When he next had a spare five minutes to talk to her, she was already gone for the day. By the time Dewey was ready to punch out at seven-thirty, he was noticeably pre-occupied. He said good-bye to everyone with a smile, but inside he couldn't get Megumi's statements out of his head. Why had she brought up the topic? Was she trying to cock-block Bibi, because she had the hots for him? That was what women did, right? Brought down the other woman to build themselves up, right? That must be it. Megumi wanted him, and this was evidence of that. It would make the Golden Week vacation interesting.

But on the train ride home he thought about Bibi. What if she was cheating on him? That might be what Megumi had alluded to, but didn't think it was her place to come out and say. She was his coworker. It wasn't her place to comment on his relationships. Japanese people almost never mentioned their significant others at work. They considered the job to be their second family. It would seem like cheating to put one's real family ahead of work. That's why Megumi's father had left the family behind and gone to work in Akita.

He got back to the guest house in Sangenjaya. Lay on the bed for a while. He had eighty-five minutes before Bibi's shift at Kawasaki ended. He knew this because she was always griping about the student she had to teach. A young man who worked at the Ikea in Shin-Yokohama. Why would she cheat on him? Maybe she'd met another teacher? There was only one way to settle this. He put on his coat and grabbed his new Canon 5D camera. It was top of the line. With an expensive telephoto lens. The kind birdwatchers and private detectives used.

He stopped at the 100 Yen store and bought a pack of gauze surgical masks. Ripped open the package and put one on. He caught his reflection in one of the mirrors. The kind the city engineers placed on poles for drivers, at the end of streets with poor visibility. With his black hair, he really did look Japanese. Then he got on the Den-en-Toshi line. In forty minutes he'd be at Kawasaki station.

23

The second floor of the Excelsior coffee shop had a perfect view of the building. Dewey sat there, cradling a medium-sized mug of hot chocolate. The ABC school was on the second floor of an office building. For the most part few people went in and out. Except every half hour when there was a small exodus of people leaving their shifts for the night. Heading to the train station.

There were two reasons you would visit Kawasaki outside of work hours. The first was for the movies. Around the station there were three multiplex cinemas. The largest of them, called the Cinecitta, was instrumental in promoting non-Hollywood studio films. It was in the middle of a shopping and restaurant area that reminded Dewey of Disneyland.

All of this was southeast of the station. The northeast was where you'd find the second reason to come to Kawasaki. The 'pink' neighborhood. The soaplands, with tuxedoed touts outside. Interspersed between the other hostess bars and love hotels.

At half past nine he saw Bibi emerge from the ABC building. A Japanese man in a suit approached her and they walked together. Away from the station. Dewey put the surgical mask over his face and headed out as fast as possible without running. He followed Bibi and her Japanese friend in the direction of the love hotels. All of Dewey's worst nightmares were coming true.

Then they went into a Chinese restaurant.

Dewey's heart slowed down. He pulled into a small building across the street. There was an open stairway next to the elevator. A common design in Japan. He walked up to the first floor landing he came to and sat down. Took out his camera. Snapped some pictures of the two sitting down.

For a moment Dewey felt a pang of guilt. This kind of behavior was creepy. In the end, he might be proved wrong. Maybe he was reading the situation in the worst way possible. Perhaps this guy was just having a Swedish lesson over mabou doufu. But he just had to know. Megumi must have known. Otherwise, why would she have dropped hints? Of course, he was often accused, even after five years in Japan, of misreading intentions.

Half an hour passed. He wanted to leave. His ass was getting sore sitting on the steps. This must look strange, him waiting. There weren't many people passing by, but he rarely saw Japanese people sitting on stairs that led to the outside of a building. Would they notice him? He was probably being paranoid.

Something caught Dewey's eye inside the restaurant. Bibi and the man in the suit. The two of them stood up and walked to the register. Paid the bill. Dewey zoomed in real tight. The extra money spent on the lens was worth it. He snapped away, following the two figures across the street.

Then he saw the bright pink sign. Coming right into frame. As they moved out of profile, it was clear they were holding hands. Bibi led the guy into the hotel. Dewey felt tears welling up. He snapped away as they went inside. He stayed there, holding up the camera like a shield.

Five minutes passed. Dewey could bear it no more. He put the camera back in his carry bag. It would attract attention. There were lots of Yakuza about. He stood up and walked across the street. But there were no windows on the front of the building. Dewey circled around back. It was a large city block. The hotel was squeezed in between several apartments and other hotels, all backing onto the train tracks. He had to count the buildings to make sure he'd reached the correct one. To the right, the hotel was flush against the neighboring apartment building. On the other side was the fire escape.

The alley was narrow and dimly lit. He had to squeeze sideways to fit. He climbed over a rumbling air conditioner. Moved as far forward as possible. He sat there, under the window. In the background he heard water running. Then muffled voices. Too indistinct.

Then came a sexual yelp. "Yeah…ah, yeah." More vocalizations of pleasure followed.

It could only be Bibi. Yeah was 'yes' in Swedish. There was no way a Japanese girl would yell that. The screams and moaning were different. But there was no question it was her.

He closed his eyes in an effort to fight back tears. But it was no good. Everything was crashing down. He'd felt something for this girl. She was beautiful. Maybe he had been dating above his station, but so what? He didn't deserve this.

Dewey was wiping the tears out of his eyes when he was yanked backwards.

The tug was violent and abrupt. The man leaned up and whispered in his ear a staccato string of Japanese words. Dewey understood none of them, except 'chikan', the Japanese word for pervert. He dragged Dewey over the air conditioning unit, smashing Dewey's thigh. There would be one hell of a bruise there tomorrow.

The man tossed Dewey into the street. Then stood silently, arms folded across his chest as Dewey got back on his feet.

24

Neapolitan-style pizza had become all the rage in Japan. In Ebisu there were five different restaurants. One of them, according to a Canadian colleague of Dewey's who lived in the area, was considered the best in all Japan. The menu was also fantastically simple. Only two kinds of pizza.

The place was on Meiji Dori, in Hiroo, the neighborhood adjacent to Ebisu known for its wealthy foreign residents. Dewey had made reservations for dinner service, but kept Bibi waiting half an hour. When he walked in, the staff took his coat. Directing him to a table near the wall.

"Did you get delayed?" she asked.

"Yes, terrible delays on the Den-en-Toshi Line."

"I was going to order without you."

"How was your day?"

"Okay. The Ikea class isn't making much progress."

"Too bad." Dewey didn't drop a hint. He wanted her to relax. Better for her reaction when the trap was sprung.

They ate a dinner of thin-crusted pizza with salad, and downed an overpriced bottle of German wine. Then walked hand in hand back to the train station.

"Let's go to a hotel," said Dewey.

"Why? We both have apartments."

"I feel like a change. Someplace special to fuck."

Bibi laughed. "If you're paying."

"In Japan, the man always pays for the hotel."

"Really?"

"Yup."

"Where do you want to go?"

"The 'stay' rates in Shibuya are reasonable."

"The place with all the hotels on the hill?"

"That's it."

Love Hotel Hill, as it was called, was up the Dogenzaka Slope from the Bunkamura. That was the complex that housed the luxurious Tokyu department store. The basement was a performance space and art gallery. The eighth and ninth floors held concert halls. And movie theaters that showed mostly snobby films from Europe that looked incredibly boring to Dewey.

So it was surprising when he discovered Love Hotel Hill was just across the street from this capital of culture.

He led Bibi by the hand.

"Where are we going?"

Dewey stopped next to a hotel with a tropical theme. "This looks good."

They made it to the room successfully, without any miscommunication with the monolingual desk clerk.

"Why don't you take a shower first? I'll join you in a second."

"Okay," said Bibi, disrobing.

Dewey took out his camera. Set it to movie mode. Walked into the bathroom. He filmed about twenty seconds of Bibi before she noticed.

"Put it away."

"I want it as a memento."

She took the showerhead in her hand and directed its spray towards the camera. Dewey ran back to the bedroom.

A few minutes later he joined her, sans camera.

"What do you want to do? Put it on the internet?"

Dewey didn't say anything. Later, when they were making love, he fantasized about Megumi.

After they were done, Bibi picked up the camera from the table.

"What are you doing?"

"Deleting the video of me."

Dewey took it out of her hands. "It's quite expensive. Shoots amazing photos, too." He flicked through the menu until he came to the recording made outside the Kawasaki love hotel. "And audio. Take a listen."

It started with the hum of the air conditioner unit. But gradually, over the grainy grey punctuated by the off kilter amber rectangle of a window, the moans started.

Bibi looked at Dewey warily. "What is this?"

"It's you. In Kawasaki after work the other night."

Bibi jumped up from the bed. "What the fuck? It's fucking gross. Is this your new hobby? Stalking me?"

143

Dewey shook his head in amazement. "I'm the aggrieved party here, you selfish bitch."

"How did you find out about this relationship?"

"From someone in the know."

"Who?"

"It's not important."

"Tell me."

"Well everyone at work seems to know about your comings and goings."

Bibi lay back on the bed. It was finally coming home to roost. What she'd got herself into when she moved to Japan. She had been seduced by Tokyo. It was the largest city in the world. How could she not be anonymous here? she had thought. But that was far from the case. She was under scrutiny at all times. Was she the enemy? Even if people didn't think that, it was all the same in the end for her.

"Fine," she said. "Tell me what you want me to do."

"I want to know if you love me."

She didn't answer.

"Well?"

"I guess so," she said, gazing at the foot of the bed.

"What the fuck kind of answer is that? I'm not insisting on it. I just want to know if this is a one-off, or if you want to break up with me. Don't keep me around out of guilt."

Bibi didn't say anything. She sat curled up in silence as Dewey got dressed.

When he was fully clothed, he walked over to her. "Do you see that door? If I walk out, there's no going back. Now, I'll ask you one more time. Do you love me?"

Bibi closed her eyes. "I'm not sure."

144

Dewey took out his wallet. Tossed two ten thousand yen notes on the bed. "That should cover the room. As long as you get out by ten tomorrow morning. With the rest of the clientele." He walked to the door connecting to the genkan. "And give my number to Yuko or Megumi. Get in touch with me through them. If you see me at work, smile politely and move on. I don't want to talk to you until we meet at Kita-Yamanouchi. There I'll pretend that we're getting along, for the sake of our coworkers."

Bibi wanted to scream. He had all the bases covered, didn't he?

But she didn't. She stayed quiet as he walked out, slamming the door behind him.

PART
SIX
GOLDEN
WEEK

25

One of the downsides of working at the ABC Language Academy, at least for the Japanese staff, was that the instructors got longer vacations than everyone else. The staff had spent the morning cleaning up the classrooms and filing paperwork. Most of them had left for a sales seminar at lunchtime, leaving only Megumi and XX until four o'clock. Fortunately, Bibi was pulling a favor for a student who would be out of the country after the holidays. She was being paid triple overtime for coming in on her day off.

Megumi was on the phone with the wife of a doctor in Totsuka. The woman and her husband were monster parents. One of the few English phrases to not be ravaged by the Japanese tendency to misuse foreign loan words. The two of them were convinced that their little brat of a kid absolutely needed to be taking an English class. Their son had kicked one of the other students in the face during a group lesson. They asked the parents to put him in private classes. The only problem was neither of the parents made sure he showed up. The previous week one of the teachers had found him playing hooky by the station. It was obvious that the kid didn't want to be here. Megumi was in mid-sentence when the mother put her on hold.

XX walked by. "When you have a moment, could you sort the student evaluations in room 301? Make sure they are hole punched, too?"

Megumi nodded. She still tried to avoid conversation with XX. There were forty-five minutes until four o'clock.

Much to Megumi's relief, working in Yokohama hadn't been the nightmare she'd feared. But this was only the first week. XX was headed to Thailand for four days. So maybe he would get his hooker fill over there. Rather than bother Megumi. Still, there was a rumor about XX and the girl who came in part time in the mornings.

After three long minutes the woman came back on the line. Muttered excuses about her ailing mother, and asked that they continue the conversation after the holidays.

Megumi hung up the phone and gazed around the curiously deserted school. The front desk was at the center of a maze of corridors that branched out. She got up and walked to 301, her ears listening for XX's presence. If he wanted to grab her, now was the time. Would he really be that bold? With other staff coming back? There was no way. She was being overly suspicious. He was obviously embarrassed by his behavior. That was why she'd been working here a week now and XX had barely spoken to her.

She arrived at the room. It was silent, except for the sound of Bibi drilling a Swedish dialog in the next room. Megumi saw three piles of neatly stacked papers, all fresh from the photocopier. Next to the hole punch was a pile of clear file folders.

She remembered Dewey complaining about Japanese hole punches. Something about how in America the paper size was bigger, so they used three ring binders. Which struck Megumi as pointless. Two rings were more than adequate. She grabbed a sheet from each pile, checked to see that they matched, and whole punched them. Put them into the clear folders.

Then she heard the breathing. From the corner of the room. The corner obscured from the hallway. Megumi looked up, startled.

She saw the giraffe first. It was standard issue, the exact same toy in all of the ABC Company's children's classrooms. They kept a collection of toys for the teacher to play games. It was fat around the waste, with a long, slender neck about the size of a sausage. Then her eyes glanced to the ground. XX had undone his pants. Pulled them down. They were down around his ankles with his white underwear. He pulled the toy giraffe aside.

XX was jacking off in front of her.

For an instant Megumi almost burst out laughing. Why the giraffe? How would that play into his excuse if he got caught? Then she realized this was his plan. The perfect entrapment. He figured he'd get away with exposing himself because Megumi wouldn't scream within earshot of a customer.

Anger rose inside of her. For a moment she stood there, like a deer in headlights, watching him. Then she reached down.

The hole punch wasn't even that heavy. Most of the handle was made of plastic. But the bottom, which rested on the table, was metal. With sharp corners. Grabbing it, she walked around to XX and slammed it into his genitals. Then she pulled it back and slammed it in again. She hit something solid. Then left the hole punch on the table and scurried out of the room.

She got back to the front desk and sat down. Looked at the clock. How long would it be before XX emerged? Maybe this would be her last vacation with the company. Oh, well. She was still old enough to get a working holiday visa. Go off and see the world.

And it would have the added bonus that she'd never have to talk to the monster parents from Totsuka ever again.

26

This was going to be an awkward discussion. Yuko should have mentioned it weeks ago. It was two days before she had to go away to Akita, and she had to tell Yujirou where she'd be. After her last day at work before the vacation, they had gone to a love hotel in Fujisawa. Yujirou had proposed spending the rest of Golden Week in the same room. Something Yuko thought was romantic, even if batshit insane.

"But why are you more interested in foreigners than me?" said Yujirou.

Yuko was surprised by this response. After all, he had lived in California. He wasn't the racist type. "You're getting all jealous." She smiled. "You really like me that much, don't you?"

"I don't understand why you waited so long to tell me. It's like you were hiding your plans."

Yuko had seen this kind of thing rear its head before. Her working at an eikaiwa had been an issue with a systems engineer she'd dated. A certain type of man that existed in all countries these days. It was just that in Japan, they took the whole thing a bit further.

In foreign countries, many people have heard the word otaku. She had met many teachers who admitted to being 'otaku' when they introduced themselves. But in Japan the term gained popularity when it was used to describe a socially isolated loner who raped and murdered the seven-year-old daughter of his neighbors in the early eighties. Since then, it has been used mostly in a derogatory fashion, to describe sexually unappealing males, many who frequent the Akihabara section of Tokyo. Obsessed with Japanese animation and degrading pornography.

Fortunately for Yuko, Yujirou's quirks stopped at socially inept. It wasn't like she'd ever caught him jerking off to cartoons, or watching scat porn.

From her purse she produced a Nintendo DS. She always carried it with her. "Let's play Tomodachi Life."

They hooked up their game devices and wandered through the world together, but Yuko raised an eyebrow when she saw Yujirou asking out one of the other female characters.

"No, stop talking to her."

"She's cute."

Yuko slapped him playfully on the arm, but he persisted.

"I've always wanted to date a member of AKB48."

"Is that who it is?"

"Yes," he said, as the woman refused his request and scampered off.

"But what about me?" Yuko put her arms around him.

"Well, you don't tell me anything. About who you are."

"I want to be your wife." She bent down and kissed his crotch.

Yujirou stroked her inner thighs. "I want someone who is loyal."

"I'm loyal."

"And I'd never cheat on you, either," he said. "Have you ever dated your foreign co-workers?"

"Once. But he dumped me."

"Did you have sex with him?"

Yuko smiled. "It's a secret."

He pushed her away. Yuko scowled. "Did you ever go out with any girls in California?"

"It's a secret," he said, grinning. He took her hand, pulling her body over his. "You mentioned that wedding hall in Aoyama? The one near Omotosando Hills?"

"Yes."

"We can book it."

"But it's so expensive."

"For you it's worth it."

She smiled. "But I have to go to Akita. I promised my Swedish coworker. She wants to have a true Japanese experience."

"Akita is boring. Just bathtub races and blizzards."

"Bathtub what?"

"They have a race. Every Golden Week. At a shrine somewhere up there. In a pond." He stroked her hair. "Stay here. With me."

"It's the money. I paid for it before I met you."

"I'll pay them back."

"And I promised to go with them. It would be weird to back out two days before. They need me to drive, too. And find the campsite."

"Well, be careful. There are crazy people in those woods."

"Like who?"

"Onibaba."

"She slapped his face, playfully. You are like a little child. So superstitious."

27

The beach was fucking ghastly. While the water was nice, everywhere the ground was littered with dark seaweed mixed with garbage. It was a narrow strip of sand between a breakwater and the Sea of Japan. The concrete barrier was about four meters high. Dewey imagined it might stop a low level Tsunami, but it would be useless against a wave like the one that hit the Fukushima power plant. Of course, that kind of event only happened once every thousand years. An earthquake like that wasn't going to hit Kita-Yamanouchi in Dewey's lifetime.

But he had to admit, Kita-Yamanouchi was located in a dangerous spot. The town had been built on a stretch of flat land. Situated between two sheer cliffs. He walked to the far end of the beach. It ended at a wall of rock, jutting over the water. Even though the nearby hills were covered in vegetation, the incline was almost ninety degrees. You couldn't hike up, you'd have to climb.

Then there was the issue that the town was a dead end. Both the main road and the train line terminated at the water. The only access to the outside world was through a tunnel. One side for the trains. Then a concrete barrier. Dividing the tracks from a narrow two-lane road. It was a marvel of engineering. But one rockslide and the town would only be accessible by boat.

At the other end of the beach was a dock. A few fishing boats were moored, but there didn't seem to be much action going on. Dewey found a bench bolted into the concrete lip of the breakwater and sat down. It was a nice day. Cloudy, but not too hot. An excellent day for hiking. Or camping. But he was not looking forward to seeing Bibi again. The last three weeks had been awkward. He'd just gotten used to having a lot more free time to himself. Started boozing a lot more heavily. Staying home. Drinking half-liter cans of lemon chu-hi. Binge watching episodes of QI on YouTube. Quite the life. This seemed to be where things were heading for him. He was a guy who did the same job day-in and day-out. Despite the fact that he only worked thirty hours a week. While waiting for time to pass between vacations. Counting the days until he wouldn't have to put on a happy face for people he wasn't interested in.

An old man walked by. He took one look at Dewey and stopped. He adjusted his glasses, then walked toward the log. "You are a foreigner," he said, in English.

Dewey smiled. "Your accent is almost perfect."

"Thank you. It took an old man like me a lot of practice. Everyone wants to speak English here. Are you on vacation?"

"Just for a couple of days."

"Are you coming to the two day march?"

"Um, sorry. I've got plans."

"That is understandable. It will be very growling."

"Grueling, you mean?"

"Yes. Very few will make it to the end."

"Yeah, these hills have quite the slope."

The man looked up towards the sky. "Yes, many have died in the mountains. But you must also be careful on the beach."

"Why?"

"The winter tides are dangerous. Many have been swept away sitting where you are."

Dewey was aware of how awful the winters were up here. One of his coworkers had married a girl from Akita. The guy had taken a few days off to visit her parents. In the middle of February. He was in for a shock. It rarely snows during winter in Tokyo. But in Akita, despite being only a few degrees colder, the snowfall doesn't stop. Her parents owned a parking lot in downtown Akita City, and put the guy to work shoveling it out after a big blizzard. He had just finished when the snow started again, undoing everything. Coming back to Tokyo, he had said, was like retuning to the tropics after a stint in the arctic.

"But you must also watch out for North Koreans," said the man.

"You mean getting kidnapped?"

"Yes, they have submarines. They would come up, right to the shore."

159

Dewey was well aware that Japan's relationship with Korea, and Koreans, was complicated. And not in a good way. Korea had been basically a vassal state of the old Chinese empire until it was colonized by Japan in the early twentieth century. Whether by choice or by coercion, millions of Koreans had found themselves working in Japan, mostly doing shitty jobs. After World War Two many had retuned to Korea. But before the whole mess had been sorted out, the Korean War had started, dividing up the country. The Koreans left in Japan had to decide whether to return to South Korea, controlled by Americans, or to North Korea, which was, at the time, and for several decades afterwards, much better off economically. The Japanese weren't too keen on making the Koreans citizens, since they hated immigration. But these migrants, known as Zainichi, had remained. As permanent residents. Some had identified with the South, while others with the North. The South-aligned Koreans had pretty much integrated into Japanese society. But those with sympathies for the North refused, setting up their own schools and basically their own society. Much of it based in Osaka and the Kansai area. Most of the pachinko industry was controlled by Koreans. And the yakuza. Or so it was popularly believed. Since many companies refused to hire non-ethnic Japanese. A big fucking mess was what it was.

So then, in the sixties, the North Koreans had started sending submarines to the Japanese coastline, to kidnap children off the beaches. Seemingly as retribution for Koreans brought over by Japan before the war. And wasn't that just the fucking cherry on top.

"My niece was one of them," said the old man. "In 1965. No one heard of her after that. We don't know if they killed her. Maybe she is still living in Pyongyang."

"That's terrible," said Dewey.

There was an awkward pause. "Well, I must get back," said the man. "Many preparations to do for the two day march."

Such silence was to be expected from Japanese people, especially older ones. The Korean situation was practically a taboo subject. Japanese are often reluctant to discuss their less-than-stellar history with outsiders.

Dewey stayed on the bench for another half an hour. As was typical at Japanese hotels, it was expected that he wouldn't be around from ten in the morning until four in the afternoon.

He wandered back into town, looking for a coffee shop. There wasn't even a Doutour. He would wait until the lunch hour rush was over before he investigated the options for coffee. He walked back over to the breakwater, following a path around the station. A train waited by the platform, one of the four that arrived each weekday.

The town was only barely big enough to not be called a village. At least, that was what Yuko had told him. By the station was the main street, lined with shops for about a block. Following that, the small shopping street turned into the main road. He followed it out past the residential areas, to where a few small rice paddies had been set up at the edge of town. The road curved towards the hills. Just before it hit the mountains, at the spot farthest from the shore, the road opened up to a large field where a stage

161

had been set up. Some workers were assembling a podium and chairs. Others were raising a banner over the stage that said "The first annual two day march" in Japanese. They were really making a big deal of this, thought Dewey. The field backed onto a temple. And a path that led back into the woods. Dewey followed the trail all the way around the open area.

The path rose up to the hills and he got a nice view of the entire town. Kita-Yamanouchi was small, he realized. An isolated outpost almost carved out of the cliffs. It was ruggedly beautiful, the way it was nestled into the mountains. Compared to the views he was used to in Tokyo, it was like he'd stepped into another time period. Unlike the sea of gray that Dewey had grown used to, the town was a small collection of run down buildings, punctuated by the occasional vacant lot. Not quite as depressing as Joetsu, but it was on its way there.

The path continued up the mountain, into the woods. It must be a wonderful hike, he thought, before turning back to town. He headed down a different route back to the field. A sign stated in Japanese that the open area was the designated gathering spot in case of earthquake. So everyone could die together? he wondered.

At the base of the hill Dewey found a big trapezoid-shaped object. Inspired by a science fiction movie, no doubt. The inscription was difficult for Dewey to decipher with his limited vocabulary. But it seemed to say that four thousand people had died here, some time in the nineteenth century. Some sort of tsunami. Apparently Kita-Yamanouchi wasn't the safest place to live.

Dewey headed back into town, rice fields on either side. He remembered that he still had to pay for his room. There had to be a bank around here somewhere.

It seemed the only financial institution in town was the post office, and it was closed. Except for the cash machine. It looked like a better option than the ATM at the station convenience store. He went inside. There was one machine, with a shrunken old woman peering over the display.

So Dewey waited.

And waited.

The woman was taking forever. This was not out of the ordinary for Japan.

"Please help me. I don't know what to do."

The old woman said it to the machine like it was a human being. At first Dewey didn't know what the woman was asking, but she repeated it so many times he finally figured out what she was saying. She kept repeating herself, like a broken record.

What was he supposed to do? Help her?

The fallout from such action was predictable. Police would be called. Everyone would want to know why a foreigner was trying to access the woman's bank account. Defrauding old people was epidemic in Japan. Someone would phone up, asking for money. Pretending to be the old person's child. Then give a bank account number. Dewey could easily believe the local cops would treat him suspiciously.

"Please help me."

Dewey looked at the phone receiver next to the machine. Was it wired in to the local police? The voice on the other end could be in Okinawa. He could pick it up, but it was practically guaranteed that no one on the other end spoke English. Then where would he be?

"I don't know what to do."

The door opened. A woman walked in and got in line behind him. The old lady repeated her request for help. She must have Alzheimer's or something. Why would her family have left the woman to fend for herself? Maybe she had no family. Perhaps she was just living alone, waiting to die.

The younger woman saw Dewey and approached the old lady. Dewey decided he was better off going to the ATM at the convenience store.

28

Dewey got back to the hotel around four-thirty. He had spent the last two hours at a café across the street from the Irish pub. It served tiny cups of coffee for five hundred yen, made with a drip coffeemaker that looked like it had been stolen from a chemistry lab. Despite this, the flavor of the beverage was unequivocally awful. At least the table had comfortable chairs.

He went back to his room and dropped off his backpack. A card on the side table said the communal bath was open from four-thirty. This was one of the perks of staying at a traditional ryokan. Just like this one, many had extensive onsens. The card said that this particular inn had three hot baths and one cold. There didn't seem to be any separate hour for men and women. Dewey figured they must have to rotate. Perhaps they had the times posted on the doors to the onsen.

He changed out of his clothes and into the yukata the hotel had left folded on the table for him. At the entrance to the onsen he slipped into the men's dressing room, exchanging his yukata for a small hand towel. Which, according to custom, must never fall in the bath water. He entered a room with a shower and rinsed himself off, then, fully nude, walked to the first hot bath. As he climbed in, Dewey noticed two people already there. A man and woman on the verge of middle age. As soon as he got in the water the man made some comment to the women. Both left immediately. Had he done something wrong? Dewey had no idea.

Sitting in the hot bath, he thought about Megumi. Why had she agreed to come with them? She had a boyfriend, didn't she? Dewey went through the reasons, and in the end decided it could only be because she had the hots for him. It was all very odd, given that this trip was mostly his idea. And it had all turned into a bit of a nightmare. If only he could get with her. After all, he'd been here for over three and a half years. Never once had he dated a Japanese. I mean, wasn't that a bit weird? A bit abnormal?

His thoughts drifted to Jenny, the girl he'd dated before Bibi. From Melbourne, she was skinny and pretty, a girl with refined looks. But with a boyfriend back home, whom she returned to. It had been a fun relationship. Still, Dewey had few regrets when she left to go. There hadn't been much passion.

Then there was the girl from Winnipeg, of Filipino descent. She was sweet. And fun. And very hot in bed. He might have even moved to Canada. But then she told him about the climate in Manitoba. They broke up when she left Japan. They'd been together for two years. Maybe if he'd pushed a little harder, he might have convinced her to come to California. But that was that.

Not long after was a Polish girl he'd picked up at Club Asia in Shibuya. She was crazy, but interesting. And she always had cash. The girl worked hostess bars in Roppongi, and made plenty of money at it, too. She paid for his meal countless times. They made love constantly. And then, one day she stopped responding to his texts. He kept trying to get a hold of her until messages came bouncing back to him. Maybe she went back to Poland. Or somewhere else. It made Dewey feel glum.

All this made him wonder if he was really desirable. He'd gone through some dry spells in the States, too. Just after graduation. But he hadn't given it a second thought. That particular time had been a brief period when he'd worked for a corporate video company. He had some skills with video editing from a course he'd taken back in 2000. He'd done demo reels for the company's directors. To show potential clients. But he'd only been there six months. His social life had improved dramatically once he'd quit.

Dewey felt his skin wrinkling. It was almost time for dinner. He toweled off and went back to his room to take a nap.

Dinner was served at six-thirty by the shyest girl he'd ever met. He tried to ask her name.

"Miki," she said.

"Like Mickey Mouse?"

"No," she said, a smile spreading across her face.

He eyed her body. She must have been in high school. Or college. Miki had smooth skin and a nice slender figure. Exactly the kind of girl he wished he were dating.

The spread the ryokan put on for dinner was excellent. Unagi and Rice. Soup. Along with small dishes of pickled vegetables, egg custard, and okra in some sort of sweet sauce. Shredded mountain potato porridge. A grey gelatinous cube that Dewey couldn't remember the name of. Three dishes of different mushrooms. Tempura. Then came another tray with more seafood: Squid. Steamed crab leg. Sea urchin. Three kinds of tuna. Sea bream. Grilled mackerel. Ikura and sea cucumber eggs. And Salmon.

Dewey picked up the bowl of squid.

"Is the ika always black?" he said, using the Japanese terminology. Leaning the correct words for fish and other creatures was half the battle in becoming an expert on sushi.

The girl looked at Dewey with incomprehension for a moment, before cluing in.

"Yes," she said. "The ink...is black." She was clearly frustrated by her lack of English.

"It's okay," he said in Japanese. "It all looks delicious."

She smiled, then retreated from his room.

After dinner Dewey walked around the corner to buy some chu-his. He thought about going to the Irish pub, but the room he'd had last night had burned a hole in his pocketbook. Better to be a cheap drunk.

There was a lounge on the first floor with a television. Dewey, full from dinner, sat down in one of the comfortable black leather chairs that looked like they'd been there since the mid-1960's. At least the TV was new. He flicked through the channels. Five on the regular band, and twelve more on the BS band, which he had been told was an abbreviation for "broadcast satellite." There was one station on the BS playing an English language kids show, the rest of the channels only had on reruns of programs from the main networks. He settled on a game show about guessing obscure kanji and lit a cigarette.

It was puzzling that he'd met no one else that night. That morning the lobby had been full with guests checking out. Would no one else be in town for the two day march?

When he got back to his room, the futon was rolled out for him. To think for years in college he'd believed the cheap couch-bed he'd paid three hundred dollars for was called a futon. When Dewey had first arrived in Japan, the company had set him up with an apartment. They didn't pay for it, but it allowed him to move in without paying key money or finding a guarantor. Part of his deposit was for a futon. Even though it was little more than a hundred dollars, Dewey had expected an American-style piece of furniture, the kind of single mattress couch-bed favored by budget conscious university students.

So it was much to his surprise when he found a large translucent plastic bag in the center of his room, about a meter high, in the shape of a rectangle. Inside he found a pillow and a duvet. As well as a thin rectangular pad, roughly large enough to sleep a single person comfortably. It folded up easily. He learned that in many Japanese apartments, the sleeping area doubled as a living room. In the morning the futons were gathered up and flung over a balcony railing for airing, to keep mould from building up. Just for half an hour or so. Then they were put away in the closet, until nighttime, to be laid out on tatami mat floors. Of course, nowadays plenty of people in Japan slept in beds, or lay their futons on a kind of bed-like support.

After a couple hours of bland talk shows and restaurant documentaries that were essentially program-length commercials, Dewey started to yawn. Finishing the last of the chu-hi cans, he disposed of them and walked upstairs. He was tired by the time he got into bed, and fell asleep easily.

In the middle of the night he was roused from sleep. Someone was lifting up the comforter, massaging his legs.

What the hell?

"Shhhh," said a female voice.

Dewey felt a yukata being undone. A woman's soft naked body pressing against his legs. Delicate hands reaching down and pulling off his underpants. He felt the woman's tongue over his legs. His heart was practically beating out of his chest. He reached down and stroked the woman's hair.

He tried to pull her face towards his, but she wouldn't let him. Instead she swung her body around, spreading her legs over his face. He began to lick, all over her thighs, fingering the moistness between her legs. She began to moan. His left hand felt her large pendulous breasts, and their hardened nipples. Dewey rubbed harder and faster at her clitoris, alternating with his mouth and tongue. His rubbing built and built with her louder and louder moans, until she finally squealed out. So loud. Everyone must have heard it.

The women lie on top of him for a minute, exhausted. The she buried her head in his crotch and licked his balls. Over and over. Then her tongue traced a trail to the tip of his cock. She moaned as she began to suck him off. Louder and louder, she went down faster, the moans stifled by the tip of his penis. He didn't last long, and came in her mouth. Her body tensed as he felt her swallow. Dewey lay back against the pillow, sleepy.

Her body moved over his. He was about to talk to her when he felt her pull away. The light from the hall crept in through the open door. She exited the room fully nude, her yukata trailing behind.

Dewey was too exhausted to do anything but fall asleep.

And that was that. For a couple of hours.

Dewey woke up again with a mask covering his eyes. He went to take it off when a Japanese female voice whispered in his ear, "Don't take it off. I'm ashamed." He felt hands all over his waist, pulling off his shirt. Again he felt a naked body against his. They kissed, and Dewey felt relieved to explore her body. She groaned and moaned, their hands all over each other. He felt between her legs, parted the ample mass of hair. The wetness of her pussy felt like it was going to melt the tips of his fingers.

The girl moved up, astride him. She was thinner, smaller chested. He felt his throbbing member glide into the wetness between her legs. Again and again she rubbed him, before reaching down and pushing him inside of her. He thrusted slowly, her hips matching his motions until they formed a rhythm together. When he could bear it no more he pulled out and ejaculated on her buttocks, pressing the glans against the smooth skin of her thighs.

They lie there cuddling for a few minutes. She kept a tight grip on his hands as she leaned over. They kissed deeply for some time. Then her body moved off his. When Dewey heard the sliding door close, he took off the blindfold and went back to sleep.

For a moment he had considered chasing after the girl, but exhaustion got the better of him. Consider yourself lucky, he thought to himself, and go back to bed.

29

The next day breakfast came with a smile. Miki gazed deeply into his eyes as she placed several small dishes on the table in his room. "This is just the first course," she said before departing.

He poured himself a cup of green tea and grabbed the two wooden chopsticks. He took a small dish, poured out a couple tablespoons of soy sauce, then mixed in some grated daikon. Miki returned with another tray of dishes. In all, Dewey counted fifteen small plates. There were three kinds of sashimi. Some rice and pickled cucumber. Fried sardines and grilled salmon. More snow crab. As well as eggs, sausages, and miso soup. And bowls of melon and yoghurt. It was a feast.

Miki pulled the tray away, bowing deeply before departing.

The first thing he noticed when emerging from the onsen were the banners. Along the main street people were putting up decorations for the two day march. As well as multi-colored carp streamers, which were traditional on Golden Week. Today was the first of four holidays. Tomorrow was a workday for the poor saps who couldn't get time off.

He turned the corner and immediately recognized the older woman who had checked him in. She was with another man, who Dewey assumed was her husband. They gave him a slight bow, which Dewey returned.

"Good afternoon," she said in English.

"Hello," said Dewey. "How are you?"

"Very good. The weather is wonderful today. Will you be staying with us again tonight?"

"No, I'm afraid not. Have to meet my friends in Oga later today. Your breakfast was wonderful." Dewey looked up at the sky. It looked like a storm was approaching. "Actually, could I ask you a favor?"

"Of course."

"Would it be possible to leave my bags by the front desk?"

"Certainly. You're sure you don't want to stay another night?"

"Well, I'd love to, but I have to catch the train at two-thirty."

"That's too bad," said the woman. "But you will be back on Sunday, right?"

"Yes, with my friends."

"Excellent," said the woman. "Well, we must get back to work."

Dewey nodded as the couple continued on. He wondered if they'd heard him fucking last night. The first girl had made so much noise. Dewey checked his cell phone. He had four hours to kill.

174

He decided to explore the hillside path he'd seen yesterday. It was a nice day, and the clouds seemed to hold off, over the ocean. Following the same path, he hiked up into the mountains. The trail wasn't as steep as he'd expected. The sheer drop off of the hills near the beach had given way to mountain paths that were climbable. He saw a sign that indicated the peak of Yamanouchi, the name for the area behind the town. Dewey decided that he would climb for about an hour, then head back.

Fifteen minutes later, he paused to catch his breath at a particularly steep stretch of the path. The view to the ocean was blocked by trees and foliage. He decided to move off the trail a bit to see if he could get a better sightline. Walking thirty or so feet towards the cliff, he heard what sounded like the clang of metal. Coming from a group of trees at the bottom of a nearby slope.

He moved down into the brush to find the source of the noise. Getting closer, he heard a man screaming. As Dewey approached the trees, he saw a clearing up ahead. The view was obscured, so he moved over behind some shrubs. Several figures, moving about. He tried to find a way around the trees, moving into the bushes.

Then stopped dead.

He saw ten or so men at the side of the clearing. They were all dressed in jogging pants and T-shirts. Nothing special there.

But they carried swords. Long katana swords. The men were fighting. Dewey caught sight of three bodies, piled up at the edge of the field. Completely disemboweled.

One of the men approached the bushes where Dewey stood. Got close enough that his face was easily recognized, burning itself into Dewey's memory. The man had a long red scar, running across his cheek to his ear.

Another man took out a sword. Scarface and the second guy bowed toward each other, then went at it. There were clashes of swords, then scarface landed a decisive blow, lacerating the man's neck. Scarface swung his sword again, cutting open the man's belly like it was a package of hamburger. The opponent fell over, moaning in pain. Then scarface dug his sword in again, stabbing the man in the upper chest. The moaning stopped.

Two of the guys from the group ran over, carrying the fresh corpse away, tossing it over the other three. The men chatted and joked amongst themselves, then the group departed, leaving the bodies to rot.

What the fuck?

For the next twenty minutes Dewey stood in shock, too terrified to move. Finally, he mustered up the courage to get going. There was no way the group had expected to be seen. You wouldn't normally go off the path, right? No one would suspect him of being a witness.

Dewey got back on the hiking trail, looking around in case someone was watching him. He walked back to town, not encountering a soul on his way there. There was only one thing he could do. He had to report this. It was a quadruple murder. What kind of people would do such a thing?

Part of him thought about heading out of town. Get on that train, and never come back. It was just like the old lady yesterday. Getting involved would only cause trouble. There would be a trial. He would have to take time off work. The press would publicize his company, and maybe he'd lose his job. It could become an international incident.

But the only moral thing to do was to report this.

Japan, unlike America, had small police offices everywhere, called koban. Officers still conducted patrols, on bicycles and in cars, with red lights flashing. But because it was hard to get around in lager cities, every few blocks you'd find a koban.

In Kita-Yamanouchi, the koban was right next to the Irish pub. Dewey walked in, and was greeted by a policeman. "Just a moment," said the man. "No English." The officer disappeared behind the corner. Another policeman emerged from the back room.

Dewey had made a mistake.

"What can we do for you?" said the officer in flawless English.

"Um…." Dewey was speechless. He could only look at the bright red scar running down the officer's cheek. For the policeman was the guy he saw in the woods disemboweling his opponent with a sword. Dewey's mind raced. "I've gotten lost. Could you help me find my hotel?"

Dewey backed off, almost convinced what he'd seen was a hallucination.

30

Futako-Tamagawa was as good a place as any to meet. It was just across the river from Kawasaki. At first Yuko thought about asking the other girls to meet her in Saitama, since that was closer to the Tohouku expressway. But Megumi, in a fit of inconvenience, had booked the rental car in Shibuya. At a Toyopet location closer to her apartment. Yuko had spent an hour dragging her backpack on crowded trains in the wrong direction to get there. At least the car rental agency had been efficient in checking out the vehicle. The one saving grace to a day that had not started well.

Yuko pulled the Corolla up to the exit of Futako-Tamagawa station, where Bibi and Megumi were waiting with their backpacks. "I'll open the trunk," she yelled out to them.

"It's all right," said Bibi, "we can toss them in the back. Let's just get going."

They tossed in the luggage. Megumi took the front passenger seat. "Everything went okay?"

"Yeah," said Yuko. "No problems. This was the last car they had left for the week. We were lucky." Yuko turned left, onto Kanpachi dori. The number eight ring road.

"Why don't you take the highway?" said Bibi.

"It's expensive, and slow," said Yuko. "It will take much too long."

"Longer than surface roads?"

Yuko nodded. Bibi might be smart, but she had never driven a car in Japan, thought Yuko. Or on the Shitoko. That was what people called the spider web of expressways that covered central Tokyo. It was a total nightmare.

One of the problems with the Shitoko was the fact that Tokyo sometimes got hit with major earthquakes. That may seem obvious to anyone living outside the country, but a little bit of history will underline why the Tokyo Metropolitan Expressway system is such a dire case. When Japan was given the 1964 Olympics, the Prime Minister at the time had the bright idea to build a highway network that would rival the American interstate system. But in Tokyo, there was a problem. Despite much of the metropolis being leveled in the war, the city had been rebuilt according to the traditional street network. Which had been designed, spaghetti-like, in the 1600's, to repel invaders. Straight roads were mostly non-existent. So the engineers came up with the idea to build the highways over the rivers that flowed through the city. This required all existing stream beds to be concreted over. It also prevented the highways from having more than four lanes, and forced the designers to build exit ramps that branched off the freeway from both the collector and the passing lanes. Something unheard of in the United States. As well, the design restrictions required dozens of awkward turns and tunnels, some which kept speed limits below forty kilometers (or twenty-five miles) per hour. Not to mention the fear that a major earthquake could cause the entire system to collapse, as had happened in Kobe in 1995.

This all led to a situation where people, even those whose families had lived in Tokyo for generations, regularly became lost and disorientated when they drove on the Shitoko. And there was also the cost—a single trip was priced at more than a meal at a fast food restaurant.

That was why Yuko preferred surface roads. Today traffic was light heading north. Most people would be heading west, visiting family in other parts of Japan. Plenty of people had to go back to work on Friday, as well. So that eased some of the congestion. It was still a nightmare crossing the bridge into Kawaguchi, but the Tohouku expressway was running smoothly.

Yuko turned down the radio. "Bibi," she said toward the back seat, "I didn't want to take the Shitoko because it's eight hundred yen, and we'd have to take the tunnels all the way to Shinjuku. They're slow, and they get really crowded in the morning. We wouldn't have saved much time."

"I'll keep that in mind next time I drive through the city."

Passing through Kawaguchi, the endless blocks of odd-shaped apartment buildings dissolved into neighborhoods of tightly packed houses. Finally, an hour into their journey, the suburbs gave way to fields, dotted with the occasional factory.

"It's amazing how much sprawl there is," said Bibi.

"Yes," said Yuko. "That's why Tokyo is so big. It is the largest flat area in all of Japan." They crossed a bridge into Ibaraki.

The drive was uneventful for the next hour or so. Until they passed the Koriyama interchange. Megumi opened her purse. She asked a question to Yuko in rapid fire Japanese that Bibi couldn't understand. Yuko nodded, and Megumi passed her a disposable gauze surgical mask.

"What's going on?" asked Bibi.

"We passed into Fukushima," said Megumi. "Do you want a mask?"

"What for?"

Megumi turned to Yuko, and spat out more Japanese.

"For the pollution," said Yuko. "From the nuclear plant."

"Is that still a problem?" said Bibi.

"We don't know. No one trusts the government."

Bibi took the mask and put it on. Her skin itched with moisture. Awful. The moment they crossed into Miyagi prefecture, she took it off.

As they got close to Sendai, traffic began to slow. Within twenty minutes they were in a full-blown traffic jam. Completely stopped.

When Yuko accelerated again, the car made an ungodly growl. More warning lights went on. Yuko shouted commands at Megumi, who opened the dash and fished through the papers inside. She opened a giant color map of Japan. Then got on her phone. After a brief conversation, Megumi said something to Yuko, then turned to Bibi. "Something is wrong with the car. We're going to the rental agency in Sendai to get it checked."

"So, they gave us a lemon."

"A what?"

"A lemon. Like, a car that doesn't work."

Megumi was confused. "Are you talking about oranges?"

In Japanese, Yuko chimed in to explain the idiom.

"Oh, yes," said Megumi. "This car is like a lemon."

Yuko took the next turnoff. Slowing as they cruised down the ramp. There was a grinding noise as they approached the tollbooth.

"Not good," said Bibi.

They managed to make it about the dozen or so blocks to the rental agency. Megumi went inside as Yuko and Bibi cleared their stuff out of the car. A man in a tie came out and started the engine. Popped the hood with some sort of cable that attached to his smartphone. He shook his head.

Bibi watched as he and Megumi discussed the situation. At one point Megumi began to plead with the man. He ran back inside. She turned to Bibi and Yuko. "He's giving us vouchers for the Tokyu hotel around the corner. They have no more cars today, but one will be here tomorrow."

"That's terrible," said Yuko.

"One of you will have to call Dewey," said Bibi.

Megumi was surprised by this. "Why don't you call him?"

"We broke up. Three weeks ago. He doesn't want me to talk to him."

"I'll do it," said Yuko.

Megumi grabbed her backpack, feeling a bit demoralized. The point of her going on this trip had disappeared. And now she would be stuck out in the woods for three days, possibly having to share a tent with an American she found repulsive. Not his personality, just his physical body. And his face. Actually, Dewey wasn't that bad, it was just that he believed he was better looking than he actually was. This was something she'd seen before. Foreign men who would normally be working at McDonalds or some other loser job, suddenly felt that they were hot shit. Because they were in Japan. Dewey fell into that category. They weren't as common as popular culture would have you believe, but they did exist. And Megumi didn't feel like being hit on for the next four days. She should have gone on vacation by herself.

Bibi walked over and grabbed the bags from the backseat, while Yuko popped the trunk. Bibi took one look and shook her head. "Yuko, did you bring a tent?"

"No, I thought you had one."

"I thought there was a log cabin where we were going," said Megumi. She was almost honest in her ignorance.

"No," said Bibi. "Add that to our lists for tomorrow. Before we go."

This was going to be a rough trip.

31

Dewey got back to the hotel and booked in for another night. Then he repeated to himself that what he had seen was not real. Just something weird brought on by fatigue. Or an acid flashback.

By the time he left to go out drinking, he believed this.

32

To call John K fat would be polite. He was obese. And tall. Essentially the guy was a fucking tank. He didn't give his age, but by the number of wrinkles in his face, he couldn't have been younger than his early forties. Dewey had met him when he'd entered the bar an hour ago. It looked like they would be drinking buddies tonight.

"But you may be surprised," he said, "that I used to be a cop in El Paso."

Dewey held his tongue. The guy was drinking a pitcher of beer. By himself. Without a glass.

"So how long you lived in Tokyo?" asked John K, punctuating the question with a huge gulp.

"Four years."

"Me, I've been here for two. Sure, living in the country, it's a bit backward. And it snows all the time up here. Hate that. Got to do all that shoveling. Even got to shovel to open the school."

"That's rough," said Dewey, sipping his pint of Rogue Amber.

"Hard to figure everything out up here. Hard to get basic information. Even though everyone in this town speaks English."

"Yeah?"

"Some pilot project the mayor has. Been really successful. Modeled on Uniqlo and those companies that want all communication in English at work. Guess the mayor's tied in pretty tight to the bureaucrats down in Kasumigaseki."

"That must be useful."

John K shook his head. "You'll never get a word out of these nips."

Nips. A racial slur that Dewey was pretty sure he hadn't heard since 1987.

"No siree. They take information and just sit on it. Everything is like a fucking knitting circle." John K spent the next five minutes in monologue, with Dewey as his sole audience member. Itemizing every reason why Japanese people were inferior to white people from the Texas-Mexico border. "But I will say, I sure do like living in Japan. Love the sushi. And the pussy."

Dewey bit his tongue, again. He didn't need to start any fights with an ex-cop. Dewey liked to think he had centrist views. But it seemed weird to him that a guy like this would want to be surrounded by people he felt were inferior. Such that he was willing to express this in earshot of a bartender who spoke perfect English.

Before Dewey could say another word, two plates of nachos arrived. All for John K, who ordered another pitcher. He did not offer to share any of his food. The cost of all this, thought Dewey. How could he afford it? Of course, for what you paid for a room in Sangenjaya you could get an entire house around here.

"So you work at the local school?"

"Well," said John K between nacho bites, "I cobble together all kinds of different things. Between kindergartens, cram schools and the high school. And I teach a class on Saturdays in Oga."

"Kindergarten. That's a lot of work."

"The job calls for lots of jumping around," he said. "I tell the mothers that this is my exercise, too." He slapped his belly. "They see my Texan-sized log rolls and laugh their heads off. They just love it."

John K stepped back from the bar, and went into a set of ten jumping jacks. When he was finished he had to wipe the sweat off his forehead. "Good exercise."

Two girls from a table at the back came up to the bar. Right next to Dewey. One was dressed in a bright neon pink skirt. Very short. The other one, a bit heavier, showed off her boobs with a tight white T-shirt.

"Why do you want to come to Kita-Yamanouchi?" asked the girl in the pink skirt.

"Oh, my friends," said Dewey. "They wanted to do some camping in the mountains. And to go to the ryokan. It's my first time staying at a traditional hotel."

189

"Really?" John K wiped his mouth. "That's all I stay at. Love sleeping on the futon. Just cause I'd always wreck mattresses back home. Had to buy a new bed every other year."

The girls ordered shouchu cocktails from the bartender, then the one in the white skirt turned to Dewey. "There are no young people in Kita-Yamanouchi. They all move to Tokyo."

Dewey smiled. "It's crowded there. Some days I wished I lived in a place like this."

The girl laughed. "There are no jobs here. Unless you are a fisherman."

The girls got their drinks and went back to their table.

John K leaned in to Dewey. "I fucked the one in the pink skirt a month ago. But don't tell anyone. It could get me in trouble."

"Why?"

"They're both in my English class at the local high school."

Dewey was taken aback. "And they get into bars?"

"Hell, no one gives a shit out here."

John K leaned over and yelled at someone in Japanese. Dewey turned around. Behind him was a short Japanese man. Wearing a giant black bearskin hat with two giant antlers attached to it. Like a Buckingham Palace guard crossed with a moose.

John K smiled. "The mayor's here."

33

The mayor had arrived with an entourage. Every single one of the old men wore powder blue fez hats, each with two small white antlers attached to the sides, and a chin strap. With matching blue sport jackets. The kind of blue that looked like it might ooze Legionnaire's disease. The local version of the Elks lodge, Dewey presumed.

"You are the foreigner," said the mayor.

"Yes," said Dewey, "I guess I am."

"Where are you from?"

"California."

"Very good. It is good to see foreign guests in our town. We want to be the first all-English speaking town in Japan."

Dewey smiled. Trying to hold back sarcasm. "That's, um, interesting."

"Please, speak English with us."

"I will."

The man nodded. "You will excuse me. My fellow members have much to plan for the two day march tomorrow." He left them, and Dewey felt relieved. A feeling that was short lived, as the door opened and a crowd of loud young girls entered. They flooded the bar, spreading out. Each occupying a different table of blue-jacketed old men. A lot of them were good looking. All were dressed in short skirts, many with tight fitting tops.

"They get paid," said John K.

"For what?"

"Conversation. To flatter the men."

"You're saying this place is a hostess bar?"

"Not exactly. There aren't any snack bars in the town here, so the owner holds special nights once or twice a week."

When Dewey first came to Japan he had seen the word "snack" everywhere. Sometimes in katakana, often in English. They were all small establishments, usually with three or four seats at the bar, and a couch or a couple of tables in the back. Many of them had a pretty good karaoke set up. Sometimes they were at ground level, but more often you could find entire buildings of them, with ten or twenty on a single floor. And while they served small amounts of food, they weren't a lunch counter. Not even close. Rather, they were small time hostess bars. With one or two girls to entertain four or five men. Provide them with conversation. All for a rather exorbitant fee. Dewey didn't get it. But then he would never pay a woman just to converse with him.

The mayor finished doing the rounds of the tables and returned to the bar, standing right next to Dewey. "You are our honored guest. I want to buy you a drink."

"Really, there's no need...."

John K shook his head. "You don't refuse the mayor. Could be dangerous."

The bartender produced a line of shot glasses and a giant tequila bottle. The good stuff. Patrón.

"Well," said Dewey, "if you insist."

"Great!" said the man. "We have heard you were in town. That is why we want to make you our honorary mayor."

"You don't need to—"

"He'd love to," said John K, rolling his eyes at Dewey.

The mayor smiled. "I'm absolutely delighted." He then turned to an old man that had appeared at his right. Spouted out an assault of rapid-fire commands. From his pocket he produced a wad of cash. Passed it to the bartender, who promptly rang a loud bell above his head. "It's time to party!" he screamed in time with the clanging.

All of the girls shrieked in response.

The sound system, previously playing low-level jazz, boomed. With music from the nineteen eighties. Dewey didn't know what it was at first, until he realized the voice belonged to Phil Collins. Something Happened on the Way to Heaven. A.M. radio knew no bounds. All of the young high school girls got up on top of the tables and started to dance. Dewey expected them to start stripping, but that was probably a bridge too far, even for this place. Then the bartender launched into a juggling routine with two of the servers. It was like the circus had arrived in town.

Dewey felt inside his jacket pocket. Found his pack of Marlborough Lights. It was empty. He looked over at John K. The guy seemed to be immersed in the dancing and juggling, already downing yet another pitcher of beer.

"Hey Dewey, do you need cigarettes?"

It was the bartender. Dewey had no idea how he knew his name. "Yeah. Do you sell them?"

"No, but one of the girls can go get them for—"

"It's okay. I need a breath of fresh air anyway."

And a break from the Elks.

34

The street outside the pub was completely deserted. What a contrast to Tokyo. Dewey's cell phone said half past eight, but it could have been three in the morning anywhere else in Japan. He walked to the 7-11 and bought cigarettes without incident. But somehow on the way back he got disorientated. He was half in the bag—and his sense of direction wasn't so keen when he was fully sober, either.

He turned left, which he thought was the right way. The Irish pub did not appear.

The headlights came out of nowhere. A red Honda minivan. It sped past, brushing his arm. At high speed. The driver obviously didn't give a shit. Normally Dewey would have simply walked on, but John K's behavior had annoyed him. Now this idiot was in a rush. Why? Where were they going on a Thursday night during Golden Week? In the middle of nowhere? He broke into a sprint. Energized by anger.

Dewey remembered the time he'd visited Miyazaki. He was walking down one of the city's wide streets. Searching for a park famous for primitive statues. On the way there, he took the main road out of the downtown. It wasn't that busy, but he watched as a car, turning right in front of him, came to a dead stop in the oncoming lane. While the driver examined a map to see if they were heading onto the correct side street. Or then there was the time he was wandering through Ebisu in the middle of the night, as taxis passed by without headlights on. At high speed. Or the entire population of Nagoya. Pedestrians living in terror of death by Toyota. No, Japan was not a country of highly talented drivers.

Dewey turned a corner and found the red van that had just nearly run him over. Parked in front of a normal Japanese house, the front door wide open to the genkan. The van was still running. He walked over.

The car was filled up with kids in the back seat. The front was empty. Dewey peered into the back window, shocking the three young children sitting on the other side of the glass. They screamed, tapping on the shoulder of an elderly man and another women sitting in the middle row of seats. Dewey pulled back.

A woman appeared in the open door of the house. Guiding out an elderly woman with a walker.

"Excuse me," said Dewey in Japanese, "are you driving that car?"

The woman didn't respond, just kept leading the woman out to the car.

Dewey switched to English. That usually got people's attention in Japan. "Look, lady, you nearly ran me over. What the fuck is so important—"

The woman looked up at him, shocked to see a foreigner.

"You have to leave, now," she said in English. "The march. It will kill you. THEY will kill you."

Dewey shook his head. The woman got the old lady into the car. "You're fucking crazy."

"Go," she said, "before it's too late."

35

The rattling of the window woke Dewey. The entire building began to shake violently. Ten seconds later it was over. Silence. A thunderclap split the air. For a moment Dewey feared the worst. But nothing happened. If there really was a problem, the tsunami alarms would have gone off, right?

He got up and searched his backpack for a bottle of water. It had been a rough night. He remembered returning to the bar for a couple of drinks. Then John K ditched him. So rather than hang around with the Elks he'd gone back to the hotel. Now he was paying the price. He really hoped he wouldn't hurl.

A couple of hours passed. Dewey couldn't get back to sleep, so he dozed in a semi-inebriated state.

At nine-thirty the room phone rang. They wanted to send up his breakfast. He felt a bit better. Told them that was fine.

Coming back from the bathroom, Dewey bumped into the woman who ran the place. "Did you feel the earthquake this morning?"

"Yes," said the old woman. "It's been a big problem. The train to Oga is completely stopped."

"Oh, no," said Dewey.

He took out his phone. The weather office website had earthquake updates. But he couldn't get a signal. "Is the internet working?"

"No," she said, "all telephones and internet are down. Only the power and gas are still working. And water."

"How long before the tunnel is cleared?"

"Probably at least a day. You're not used to this in Tokyo?"

Dewey shook his head.

"It happens a lot. The government must spend much money keeping the road open. Especially in the wintertime. There has been talk. They want all of us to leave. I hope not."

"Why? It's such a nice place."

"It is so far away. And expensive to maintain the tunnel. It is several kilometers to the next station. At least once a year there is a collapse."

"Has anyone been hurt?"

The woman nodded slightly, but stayed silent.

Miki yelled something in Japanese from the hall.

"Your breakfast is ready."

"Great," said Dewey. His stomach was queasy. But grease might help. If they had any grease in the sushi.

Breakfast was different this morning. Almost no fish. Fortunately. Maybe the people felt sympathy for him. They had set out a breakfast of steak, eggs, three kinds of toast and muffins. French fries. And mochi, the ubiquitous cakes made from processed rice gluten. Along with fruit salad and strong coffee.

There was no use worrying about it. He packed his backpack with the assumption he would be leaving this afternoon. No point worrying while on vacation. He had almost finished tidying up when there was a knock on the door.

It was the woman who ran the ryokan. "If you need to stay because of the tunnel collapse, we'll give you a big discount. If you buy your own food."

"That would be great. Thanks." He bowed deeply and left the room. The only thing he could do now was head to a café and read his book. Maybe go to the beach again.

Passing through the lobby, Dewey was surprised that not a single other guest was around. Surely someone else had been delayed as well?

He nodded to the old man watching the desk and headed for the exit. Dewey slid the front door open. And was confronted by a crowd.

"We have been waiting for you," said the mayor, now wearing a ten-gallon hat. He beckoned to two men over at his left. They approached with a pole and a banner. "As our honorary mayor, we would be pleased if you led the parade to the stage."

"Um, ah…."

Through the crowd, John K appeared. He didn't look the slightest bit hung over. Dewey looked at him. John K gave

201

him a nod, as if to say, just humor them, this will all be over in an hour.

Dewey sighed. He didn't have any excuse to refuse. The train wasn't coming any time soon. He reached over and grabbed the banner. The mayor raised his hands and everyone cheered.

"Later today I have to leave. When the tunnel is cleared."

The mayor just laughed.

36

One of the old men, in a surprisingly spry display, ran up to Dewey with a cowboy hat. It seemed like they'd be disappointed if he didn't wear it, so he put it on. Not that anything else alluded to a cowboy theme.

"There, you're all ready to roll out," said John K.

"Actually I was planning to—"

"Now," said the mayor, "you are able to do my job." He turned around and motioned to a brass marching band, that looked straight out of an American high school football game. Uniforms with tassels and everything. They raised their instruments to their lips.

"Is this for real?" asked Dewey.

"Very real," said John K.

Their instruments produced a horrible droning noise.

After a moment it began to organize itself into an off-key melody. The band had five horn players, a saxophonist, plus a drummer. Possibly this was their first attempt to play together.

The mayor grabbed Dewey and led the procession off, all along the main road. They turned, heading toward the mountains.

"What an honor it is to have a foreigner as an honorary mayor today."

"You could have given the job to John K."

"He is fat. That wouldn't look good in the publicity photos."

"I don't understand."

"We want this to be remembered as a day when the strong have triumphed. You are strong looking. It gives our event a sense of legitimacy."

"What event?"

"The two day march."

"Which is what? Some kind of marathon?"

"It is a competition. Where we see who can survive the longest."

"Uh-huh. Where?"

"In those mountains."

"Won't it be dangerous, with the earthquake, and the rockslides?"

"The more danger, all the better."

"Well, if the train makes it in by two I'll have to leave."

The mayor didn't respond, just kept grinning.

The procession reached the vacant lot at the edge of town. The stage Dewey had seen yesterday was now decorated with flowers and carp streamers. In the middle of the stage was a "hiro-no-maru', the Japanese flag. Except they were using the wartime variation, with the stripes. As they got closer to the platform, it began to dominate Dewey's entire field of view. Off to the side, tents had been set up. He could smell the oil frying. Probably yakisoba. And some sort of fried squid. Maybe fried chicken balls, too.

On the stage stood what Dewey assumed was a Shinto priest, with two assistants. When Dewey got there, a young man grabbed the pole and streamer from him. The mayor led them up, directing where to sit down. He looked out over the field. For fuck's sake, thought Dewey, the whole town's here. Spread out in front of the stage was a crowd of thousands.

John K reappeared. Sat down next to Dewey. "Whatever you do, don't run away."

"Huh?"

"It could cause problems."

"Like what."

"They might kill us."

Dewey looked at him. The statement had been uttered so casually that it sounded like he was joking. "What is going on?"

"This is their way of dealing with things. Just go with the flow."

"Why?"

"If you do, you'll never have to worry about money again."

"How?"

"Compensation payments." John K looked around, to see if anyone was watching. "They've been told not to target us. They know it will look bad. Just stay calm."

The priest, a man dressed in a traditional garb and horn-rimmed glasses, unfurled a scroll. He then addressed the crowd in a drone of Japanese. Dewey didn't understand a word of it.

The mayor started clapping. The crowd followed. The priest bowed deeply and handed the scroll to the mayor. Holding out some kind of plant leaves Dewey couldn't identify, the priest walked over and blessed the town officials.

Then the mayor nudged Dewey with the scroll. "It was written for this very event. Impressive, isn't it?"

"Um, yeah, I guess."

The mayor beamed. "We had to give his shrine quite the donation to get him to come, but I think it was worth it. The gods will be happy with us."

The priest finished. Everyone went silent as he left the stage. Got into a waiting Toyota Crown and drove off.

"Why all the silence?" asked Dewey.

"We do not want him to bear witness to what must happen next."

37

Dewey hadn't noticed the tables on the way in.

People were lined up. Each table was manned by old ladies with two piles of armbands. One of the bands was red, printed with the kanji for old person. The other armband was yellow.

Further back, children and teenagers were assembled. Each of the older ones had to produce a student card, which was noted by an old woman with a clipboard.

Dewey leaned over to John K. "What is going on?"

"They're separating people. Children aren't allowed to participate in the march."

"Why not?"

"You'll see. It will become very clear in a few moments."

Japan was a bit of a culture shock for Americans. Especially when they talked about age. Dewey had felt it. Living on your own was the big difference. Back home it was expected that you'd leave home at eighteen. That wasn't the way it worked in the rest of the world. Especially not in Japan. Many people got married and they still lived with their parents. Hell, he knew many students of his who still lived at home well into their late thirties, even their forties. That was why it was so hard to buy a house. People just inherited them from their parents. Of course, the government had tried to free up land by charging a huge inheritance tax. But this wasn't enough to overcome societal inertia. It was the same reason why salarymen were often forced to transfer cities every three years. Unlike in America, few people just got up and left. Ever.

The sun was giving Dewey a splitting headache. He leaned down and grabbed the bottled water from his backpack. Took a swig. The hat was ridiculous. He took it off, wiping away the band of sweat it left with his handkerchief. It sure was warm for the last week of April. Dewey had been told Northern Honshu took longer to warm up than places further south, but this year that clearly wasn't the case.

The mayor stood up. Walked to the microphone. Dewey noticed something peculiar. He carried a case with him. Made of metal.

"The future," said the mayor, "starts with a strong, youthful Japan. For far too long, our country has been allowed to drift. Much of that is our fault. Well, today, we begin to take responsibility for that future." Then the mayor switched into Japanese.

Dewey began to drift into sleep. He'd had enough of giving a shit.

Then the gunshot rang out.

38

Dewey woke, startled. The mayor was by the microphone. Machine gun in hand. He was the one who had fired the bullet. Dewey looked around. Were they going to shoot him?

"Don't worry," said the mayor, coming back to his seat, "we just want you to bear witness to this."

A middle-aged man, who Dewey recognized as one of the Elks club members, stood up and went to the microphone. He read from a list. "Elderly, one thousand, seven hundred eighty-seven. Youth, two hundred sixty-seven. Adults, four hundred twenty-five."

"What the hell is that?" asked Dewey.

"They've broken everybody up," said John K. "Youth twenty and under. Elderly sixty and over. And the rest are in-between."

The children, led by the oldest high school students, formed a line, two by two. A whistle was blown. The mayor said a few words in Japanese that Dewey didn't catch. Then the procession started back to town. On the stage, everything paused. Nothing happened until the children were out of sight.

The mayor approached the microphone. "Now, to our elders, we thank you for your contributions to this town. But as you all know, we've made the decision to accept your sacrifice for the goal of giving Kita-Yamanouchi a future. I just want to say that this sacrifice will not be in vain. Those children walking back to town are your legacy. We want to see them grow up with opportunity. To live rich, abundant lives. This sacrifice today will help that."

The mayor raised the machine gun. "Do you accept to be sacrificed?"

There was a nodding of "yes" from the crowd of elderly.

"Then we will allow you to make your sacrifice." The mayor raised his weapon. "And remember, be brave. No movement until the first shots are fired, please."

Dewey stood up, but was immediately restrained by John K's fleshy hand. "Whatever happens now, don't move. You could get injured."

One of the mayor's staff yelled instructions into the microphone. Those in the yellow armbands began to move away from the front of the stage. Taking shelter off to the sides. Many of the older people in red armbands started to run for the hills. Ignoring the mayor's orders. Many, but not all.

"This gun, it is a gift from a friend of mine. An American colonel at the airbase in Atsugi. I was a guest at his home in

America. He trained me. Taught me how to shoot. And for that, I'm grateful."

The mayor unhooked the safety and fired.

A line of elderly in the front of the stage took the brunt of the ammunition. Instantly cutting them down. Heads exploded. Blood ran down their faces.

Dewey shut his eyes. He was sure he was going to die. Not knowing what to do he fell to the ground, even though the mayor was right next to him.

There was no way he'd survive the onslaught.

39

The old people scrambled towards the mountain. The crowd gained speed, but there were many who couldn't run fast enough. A line of elderly, in wheelchairs and with walkers, didn't even try to move. They just stayed put, letting the machine gun bullets pour over them like rain.

The whole thing lasted less than twenty seconds.

The trigger clicked. That was the end of the magazine.

Dewey lie there, frozen in terror. These people had gone mad. What the fuck was going on here? He didn't dare move, just stood there, watching the bodies of the elderly victims. No one was helping them. No one was stopping the mayor. It was like everyone else was in on some cruel joke.

More clicking. "Help me," said the mayor, "I'm in trouble."

John K stood up. "Magazine's out. You need a new one." A young man from the back of the stage ran up. With ammunition. But the mayor was struggling to release the empty.

"Here, let me see that," said John K. He took the weapon. Pressed a leaver near the top. Nothing worked. "Ain't that the damndest thing."

"Wait," said the mayor. "Pass it to me. I remember. They had to modify it for full automatic mode." He flicked a leaver. "It needs to be put back on semi." The magazine came loose. Quickly he replaced it, and fired out on the senior citizens. But any of those who could run were already out of range.

"Well," said the mayor, "I gave it my best shot, and that's all we can ask for." He gestured to two men from the side of the stage. "All right, put them out of their misery."

Dewey recognized one of them—with the scar. The police officer. They pulled out long katana swords and walked off the stage. Began to attack the old people left behind. This was what Dewey had witnessed in the woods. A practice session. On who? Prisoners, probably. Chinese migrants held at the local jail.

Everyone waited for the bodies to be hauled away. Then tables were set up with bright colored awnings. Trucks with cooks appeared, taking out supplies. Dewey looked on as everyone on the stage stayed still, waiting for the last of the elderly corpses to be covered in blue tarps. Like they were going to be hauled away later.

The mayor spoke a few words to one of the men. Then walked up to the loudspeaker. "All right, everyone," he said in Japanese, "lunch will be served in ten minutes. Yakisoba for everyone. And tea. The march will begin in one hour."

Dewey looked around. Music started up. The site of a massacre had turned into that of a country fair. At one of the tents they were handing out free beer and shouchu. Like this was an occasion to celebrate. And the people. No one seemed fazed by it at all. Except for a couple of women. Sitting off to the side, crying. Some of their relatives must have been cut down first.

Dewey got in line for something to eat. He didn't know what else to do. John K lined up behind him.

"What is going on?" said Dewey. His state of shock was dissipating.

John K turned to him. "Lunch time. Then, into the mountains."

"To do what?"

"Kill the rest of the old people that got away."

"What?"

"Yeah. Until midnight. Then those who are left will survive until next year."

After they were given a glass of cold green tea, Dewey followed him to the next line up, like a zombie. Everything that happened for the next few minutes seemed to be out of a movie. He got a paper plate of yakisoba. John K stuck with him the entire time. Like a kind of bodyguard. He was already heading up to the stage when Dewey protested.

"I need to be in the shade."

"Why?"

"My skin. I'll burn." It was the only thing his mind would latch on to.

"Fine."

They headed back behind one of the yakisoba tents that offered a bit of respite from the hot sun. Sat down on the ground. John K gobbled up his plate of noodles like someone was about to take them away from him. Dewey just sat there, despondent.

"You knew this was going to happen?"

"Huh?"

"The massacre."

"Well," said John K, swallowing some more noodles, "this is the way it was done years ago. Send the old people up on the mountain to die. They figured it would be more humane for those who couldn't walk. Euthanasia day for the old folks."

"And what if the people on the mountain live?"

"Some might. But not many, once we're done with them."

"Excuse me?"

"After lunch we're heading up the mountain."

"I'm not going anywhere."

"Oh, yes you are. They'll make you help. Get the rest of the old people. But don't worry, this is just an experiment. If it goes well, they'll do it again next year. I'm just here to observe. And you—well, you just got lucky. They were supposed to cancel all the reservations. Someone must have made a mistake, given you the wrong room or something. Otherwise we would've had to cancel the whole thing." John K looked down at his empty plate. "I'm hungry for more. Be back in a second."

As he walked away, Dewey's mind drifted to the half-forgotten encounter with the woman driving the red minivan. The tunnel hadn't collapsed. It was a lie. There was an escape route. But would they come after him? His mind went to the police. Did they have guns? The mayor was a terrible shot. What if they shot him? They couldn't cover up his body being riddled with bullets. It was too much to think about. Too much he didn't know.

Dewey put down his plate of yakisoba and ran.

40

The sweat poured down his forehead, desperation in liquid form. The entire town was deserted. Even so, Dewey kept to the edges. He looked back to see if anyone was following. But the road behind him was empty. He kept going. The streets and houses were deserted. Everyone was at the two day march. Accounted for. He turned a corner and found the main road out of town, next to the railroad tracks. It wasn't far now. Why hadn't anyone given chase? Surely John K had told someone?

He remembered the tunnel on the way in. It had been night then. How long had the train taken to get through it? Dewey couldn't remember, but it was a long way to the outside world. Several kilometers. With no place to hide.

He reached the entrance to the tunnel. The mountain went straight up around it. He looked back again. No one was following him.

Dewey ran forward. Into complete darkness. This was going to be rough. Either the earthquake had severed the power lines, or the lights had been switched off. It didn't matter. He was running into pitch black. As the entrance grew smaller behind him, he slowed down. Walked up to the narrow sidewalk at the edge of the road. Felt the smooth concrete walls. His only guide. This would be a tortuous journey.

Headlights flicked on. Panic seized Dewey's body. A car was coming towards him. He thought about running back, but that wouldn't help. Instead he confronted the car head on. Kept to the sidewalk. The car jumped the curb, intent on blocking his path. Dewey hopped over it, jumping off the front bumper.

A man got out of the passenger seat. Started to pursue. Dewey bolted, but he was already exhausted and dehydrated. The skinny Japanese man caught up easily and tackled him around the knees. Dewey went down. His arms scraped the concrete.

The car backed up. A man got out of the backseat. Pulled out a gun. "Don't move. We will kill you if you try to escape."

Dewey sat down on the curb. He should have ran to the beach. Tried to swim out of here.

"Why did you come to this place, anyway?" asked the man with the gun. "Nobody ever visits this part of Akita. Unless they're here on business."

"I just wanted to relax."

"You picked the wrong time."

"Why? Don't you people ever go on vacation?"

The man laughed. "This is more important."

Dewey looked down at the man's weapon. "Why don't you put the gun down?"

"I have to make sure you stay put."

"How am I going to escape? You can just call your friends."

"The cell phones and radios don't transmit out of the tunnel."

Dewey turned around. Another car was coming.

Long before the lights became visible, the roar of the gas-powered engine filled the air. Turning the corner was a black Toyota Crown, identical to the one that had taken the priest away. It stopped in front of them. The mayor got out of the back seat.

"What are you doing Dewey? You are our honorary mayor. That is a very serious duty. How could you run away like this?"

Dewey stared at him. Wondering if he was going to pull out the machine gun.

"This is our culture. How disrespectful of you. You could have been hurt very badly. Maybe you don't understand. John has told you about the money, has he not?"

Dewey nodded.

"Well, please, understand that you are an important part of this process. Please do what we ask you. Then you may go on your way."

Dewey didn't believe him. But he stayed silent.

John K emerged from the back seat of the car. Dewey watched as the vehicle heaved upwards, relieved of his massive weight. He walked over and sat down on the curb, next to Dewey. "Listen, buddy. I understand this is a lot to take in, but you running out of here is getting in the way. Of everything. Okay? So just stay cool. These are serious guys, but they don't have to be."

Dewey nodded, a bit more sincerely this time.

"You'll come back with us, and not cause any trouble?"

"Okay."

When they got back underway, it was just him and John K alone, in the guard's car.

"I might still get away, you know. You can't put guards on the entire mountain."

"Are you out of your mind? There's no way out of here. It's a full-day hike in any direction. The only way down the other side of that mountain is on the main trails, where they have guards posted, or over a lake. Unless you've got climbing gear."

"Maybe you're right." But Dewey was already planning ahead. Now he knew they only had one automatic rifle. They couldn't hurt him all that badly if he escaped.

41

The first priority is to find the clearing."

Dewey was in the middle of the pack. The mayor and his bodyguards were leading the way. Trudging up the mountain. They had departed the town half an hour ago. John K and another man followed behind. Dewey turned to them. "What are you talking about?"

"They have a space," said John K, "where they can go and be immune from attack. It's somewhere at the top of the mountain. Of course, no one was told exactly where it was. You see, there are several clearings, and we don't know which one. But if we find it before they do, we can blockade it. Up our kill numbers."

"And you think they won't fight back?"

"They can't. It's the rules. None of the elderly are allowed to attack. They can only evade or hide from us. Unless they get to the designated field. Of course, it's way too small to hold all of them. Many have probably figured out our plan and right now are hiding themselves. Those people, with mental and physical resources, are the people we want to live."

Dewey shook his head. "You said we weren't getting involved."

"They had to change their minds. More old people got away than they expected. Originally they had planned to euthanize half the population at the stage. Until the gun got stuck."

Euthanize. That was what he called a massacre. "And you knew about all of this? Even at the Irish pub?"

"Well, they've got lots of dirt on me. It was best that I kept my mouth shut. Either way, I'm sure this story will have a happy ending."

Dewey didn't reply. He'd seen this before among ex-pats who'd been here a long time. The tendency to start believing what they were told. To lose their ability for critical thinking. Take orders without asking any questions. It was the only way to keep your job. But John K had only been here two years and he'd drunk the Kool-Aid. Hard to believe. Of course, he probably saw himself as an outspoken rebel. Didn't notice how he took his orders without a second guess.

The path got narrower the higher they went. After an hour they were walking single file. The next thirty minutes were straight up. It was rough on Dewey, but he got a perverse pleasure in watching John K struggle. He looked like he hadn't climbed a hill in years. Streams of sweat poured off the top of his head.

The mayor moved behind Dewey. His face had an almost-apologetic expression. "You have to understand our system. Today we kill only those over sixty. With the red armbands. If they survive until sundown, they can go free. Once night falls, the march ends for the day."

They stopped. "Over there," said the mayor to the goons, "a ribbon." Three bodyguards clambered through the brush. Found a tree with a plastic yellow ribbon wrapped around it. At the base was a large burlap sack. One of the men opened it and turned it upside down. Half a dozen machetes fell out, their shiny metal gleaming in the sunlight bleeding through the trees. Everyone was handed one.

Dewey felt the weight of the weapon in his hand. The blade was finely sharpened. As expected in Japan. The way they liked their knives. He whacked at some bushes with it. It was like he was in darkest Africa. The mayor stood in front of him, completely defenseless. This was Dewey's chance.

Two of the men got to him before his arms completed the arc. The clang of metal on metal shrieked out through the forest.

The mayor laughed. "Are you prepared to lose an arm, just to make me suffer?" He stretched his hands out to Dewey. "If it is so important for you to kill me, then go ahead. I'm fifty-nine. Next year I will be one of those with the red armbands. There is nothing I fear, not even death."

Dewey gripped his machete. But he couldn't do it.

The moment was broken by yelling. Several other men in yellow armbands stormed down the trail. Most of the town's population was ahead of them. Only the mayor, his guards and John K had been delayed by Dewey's escape attempt.

225

One of the people coming down the trail was the bartender from the Irish pub. He approached the mayor. "They've found the safe zone for the elderly."

"How far?"

"At least another hour's walk from here."

The mayor nodded. He turned to Dewey. "They cleared it out just for this event. None of us have been up here in weeks. All to prepare for this day. This is important. You will have to use your weapon."

Dewey's eyes narrowed. Like hell, he thought.

42

Twenty minutes later one of the men up ahead yelled out. They'd found a cooler just off the trail. Everyone ran up and gathered round it. Inside were sandwiches and drinks. One of the goons said they were placed all over the hill, for the yellow-arm-banded people.

Dewey was handed a bottle of water. Chilled by the ice in the cooler. The cold liquid against the inside of his mouth reminded him that his goal wasn't to stop these people, it was simply to survive.

He turned around and saw the path had a perfect view of the town, now far below. It really wasn't little more than a strip of land completely enclosed by cliffs. These hills were the only part that didn't form a completely vertical incline. They literally had to dynamite the mountain to get to the outside world. Such beauty. Now smeared with death.

Dewey sat down next to the mayor and ate a ham and cheese sandwich. "Just how do you expect me to keep people from finding out about this?"

The mayor laughed. "You do not understand the press in this country. They will never report anything that hasn't been approved by the government news agency. You and John K will be paid off. As a courtesy."

"And if I talk?"

"No one will believe you. Besides, it could be hazardous to your health."

"And the people in the town?"

"Everyone in Kita-Yamanouchi has been sworn to secrecy. This was not a decision we undertook lightly. Many meetings were held. Alternatives were discussed."

"How could you allow this to go on?" said Dewey. "Have you not a shred of moral decency in you?"

The mayor laughed. "This, from an American? Who drops bombs on Arabs and Guatemalans? Supports regimes that throw people out the backs of airplanes while still alive? It's a tough world. This is our response to it. All of this has been approved by the government. Not publicly, or officially. But it is seen as a...what is the word you use...the first kind of project...."

"A pilot project?"

"Yes. Exactly. If successful, they will continue until the government debt is under control."

"If successful? How could it fail? These are bedridden elderly."

"Like you say, if the outside world found out we were euthanizing old people en mass, they would get upset. They prefer to let the elderly die one by one. Without government help."

"And you organized all this?"

"No, no. They came from Kasumigaseki, in Tokyo. All the bureaucrats walked up this very mountain. Looked at the terrain. Found spots for people to hide. Places to put food and supplies. And weapons. Some have said this could even be practice for recruiting the elderly into the self-defense forces. What greater way could they ask to serve their country?"

"As what? Kamikaze soldiers?"

"Many governments have done so, not just Japan. Imagine if Russia had not flung its peasantry against the German front lines. Or if the Arabs stopped suicide bombers. Where would those countries be now?"

"And cell phones? You won't let anyone use them?"

"No. Some people are weak. They would bring in outside help. Cowards do that." The mayor looked off, admiring the view. "There is a crisis in this country. It is very hard to see from Roppongi or Shibuya. Tokyo has lots of rich people. Insulated from the farmers and the fishermen. Their trains all arrive on time. Restaurants always happy to serve them. A paradise on earth. In the largest city in the world. But they've never had to put up with Akita's hospitals. There is no way we can support an entire population of old people. No way. And in Japan, nothing happens until it becomes a crisis. But some of us are trying to prevent that. Give the countryside a fighting chance. That is why everyone here speaks English. They believe in Kita-Yamanouchi. The two day march is the same. Otherwise there will be nothing left of Japan but Tokyo, Osaka, and Nagoya."

"Not Fukuoka?"

"They're just a bunch of wild gangsters. Too close to Korea." The mayor took a sip of green tea. Then leaned in to whisper to Dewey. "If this goes well, we might not have the march again for another ten years. If we're lucky." The mayor stood up, walked over to one of the men in black. As Dewey watched him leave he realized the guy thought his logic was watertight. Even if it was completely batshit crazy.

Thunder cracked the air.

Dewey felt a shockwave from the ground underneath him. That wasn't an atmospheric disturbance. It was an earthquake. A big one.

43

Down the path there was a rockslide, then came the sounds of screaming. Someone had been hurt.

Around the side of the cliff the bartender caught sight of a nightgown. He yelled to the group in Japanese. Three of the men rushed over. Tried to get the woman out from under the boulder. Dewey walked over, to see if he could help. She was clearly elderly, straight out of the nursing home. It was almost comical. The woman was still breathing. They were trying to rescue her. And then what? Kill her once she could run free?

"What a mess," said the mayor. "We better leave her to die. Let the clean up teams take care of her."

"I don't know," said one of the goons, "we better take her back to the path. Otherwise the bears might have her for food."

Dewey and John K held back while the mayor and his goons decided what to do about the almost-dead woman. It turned into quite the debate. This, thought Dewey, from the man who just gunned down fifty people.

"How exactly are we going to survive out here?" asked Dewey. "I don't have a sleeping bag."

"There are supplies at the top of the mountain. It won't be luxurious, but we won't freeze to death, either." John K munched on a sandwich. His second. "All you got to think is how many you can take out. This is like a war against them old folks. Make sure they don't get away. If you don't, tomorrow will be much harder."

While John K was talking, Dewey felt his phone vibrate in his pocket. "I've got to take a leak."

"Sure thing, buddy."

Dewey had reached for the mobile instinctively, but then held back. The phone only vibrated when he got a text message. Maybe he could contact someone. He moved behind a tree, unzipping his pants like he was taking a piss. Fumbling with his hands, he got the phone out.

He wanted to leap for joy when he saw the green circle attached to the square of the text message button. He touched it.

Yuko: "Got your message. Will see you tomorrow, or whenever it clears up."

Dewey's entire body convulsed. He hadn't sent a message to her in three days. Yesterday, when the girls were delayed, they had talked on the phone. He scrolled down. Someone had texted Yuko using his account. Someone who didn't know how to use English grammar properly. Yuko must not have noticed, it not being her first language. But even in a drunken stupor he wouldn't have sent this: "Rock fall road is blocked. Will not come today. If can go tomorrow, it will go."

He scrolled up and checked the time. Six-thirty in the morning. After the quake. Someone had come into his room and sent a message from his phone. While he was sleeping away his drunken stupor. Dewey opened up the map application. It gave his exact location, and showed the path to the bridge on the other side of the mountain. The campsite was just across the lake. He had to find a way to get there. This very same trail led, eventually, to that bridge.

To the campsite the girls were staying tonight.

Dewey brought up the phone keypad. But the signal disappeared before he could dial the emergency number. He put the phone back in his pocket.

The most important thing now was to find a way to escape. There was no point heading back to town. He had to get across that river, or the lake. Or anywhere there were other people.

From there he could call for help.

44

Bibi was staring out the window at the endless rice fields. That's all she'd seen since they left Sendai. This was the rice basket of Japan. At least, the parts of it that weren't contaminated with nuclear fallout.

Megumi and Yuko were arguing about the best way to get to Akita. Megumi had tried to convince them that local roads would take less time and have lighter traffic on the holiday weekend. But Yuko was having none of it, refusing to leave the expressway. Bibi sat in the back, listening to them bicker like two parents on their way to a divorce. But she didn't feel unnerved by it. The fact that they were able to argue was, by Japanese standards, an admission that they were close, comfortable enough to disagree with each other. For Japanese coworkers, this was practically unheard of.

The argument had been preceded earlier this morning by a fight over which tent to buy at Tokyu Hands—the massive department store dedicated to stationary, lumber and sporting goods. They even had a kitchen utensil floor. Yuko had wanted to buy one big tent for all four of them, but Megumi confessed she didn't want to sleep in the same tent as Dewey. Bibi agreed. It would just be awkward for her. She had even said that if he put the moves on her, Yuko would have the best chance of fighting him off. Yuko had said nothing, but she knew that Megumi and Bibi were better looking, and faced a higher risk of Dewey getting out of hand in close quarters. It was like they were dealing with a child, not a thirty-year-old man.

Yuko turned the car onto the Akita Expressway. Megumi turned out to be right. The traffic jam had started just after they left the Tohouku Expressway section.

Megumi looked out her window. "We should have taken the old road that follows the Akita shinkansen. No one takes it."

"But it curves through the mountains," said Yuko, "and it only has two lanes."

"Sure, but that's why no one takes it. Everyone is on the highway. Even people heading to Hokkaido. They think it will save them time on the way to Aomori."

Megumi checked her phone. There was a website devoted to monitoring traffic jams. Bibi had seen it before. It was near perfect in estimating how long it would take you to get to your destination. Japan was good for that.

Megumi started up again. Almost screaming at her phone. "This is a mess. Nothing is moving."

"Well, that's understandable," said Bibi. At work the

girls were always on their best behavior. Now it seemed like non-stop anger and bickering. And this was only day one of four. Bibi didn't know what to do. Even in the easiest situations she had trouble figuring out the correct way to behave around Japanese people.

As the vehicles came to a halt, a shadow descended over the back window. Bibi turned her head around and saw a giant metal box of a van. It had been converted. With loud speakers and mesh metal grills over the windows. Like it was prepared for battle. Painted pitch black. When traffic began to move, she caught a glimpse of the driver, and another man, in a black bandanna, seated on the passenger side. Above the windshield someone had tied a banner on the aerofoil, with the wartime "hiro-no-maru" flag.

The truck's speakers cracked, blasting military marching band music. So loud Bibi almost jumped out of her seat. Megumi and Yuko looked back. "Oh no," said Megumi. "Gaisen uuyoku."

"What?" said Bibi.

"Right wingers," said Yuko.

The marching band music changed to a recording of a speech. A Japanese man, yelling angrily.

"What is he saying?" said Bibi.

"The man is angry about foreigners. And the constitution. He says Japan should take control of Asia. That the government is a puppet of the Americans. And should take control of Korea and China."

"Lovely," said Bibi. She had seen these guys before, parked outside Shibuya or Shinjuku station. She had often wondered what would happen if vans like that showed up in

Times Square, in New York, giving speeches encouraging the government to invade Guatemala. Or bomb Iraq. How well would that go over?

And so it went. For another half-hour traffic crawled along, the van continuously blaring hate speech and march music. Bibi realized that the girls up front must despise her by now. The complications of bringing a white person on vacation with them. When they came to the first exit Yuko turned off the highway. Mercifully the black van didn't follow.

"Thank god," said Bibi.

"There are many of them in Saitama. Especially towards Gunma," said Yuko.

"They are awful," said Megumi. "There are many angry poor people in Japan."

Bibi slumped back in her seat. "But who runs those vans?"

"Some people think they are Zainichi Koreans," said Yuko. "To discredit the Emperor. But that is just a rumor."

At least traffic was moving on the main roads. They continued on for an hour, and it turned out that Megumi was right. Local roads were moving faster than the expressway.

Bibi couldn't help but see all these things as forebodings toward her time spent with Dewey. How would he act when he saw her? She had asked around the office, but he didn't seem to have a new girlfriend. Of course it was only a few weeks since the breakup. Which kind of made things worse. He would be horny. Or maybe vindictive. But she had arranged for this trip. She would behave like a decent human being no matter what.

"I'm glad we don't have to deal with Dewey today," said Megumi. "He can be difficult."

Yuko nodded in agreement.

45

The three of them must have been in their early nineties. They had been tied together by a line of string. All women. Right out of the nursing home.

Dewey had kept back. Watching the mayor making plans. If you saw the group of them, you'd think they were trying to sneak up on a lion. "What is with the discussion?"

"No idea," said John K. "This is practice for later in the day. I guess they want to be careful."

The women were sitting on a rock, yelling and screaming. All three victims of Alzheimer's.

The mayor and his men came back. "We have decided you two are going to help." He motioned to John K. "You go first."

"If you insist."

Dewey was aghast that John K didn't protest. He almost seemed to get excited to do some state-sponsored murder. He got up, and lumbered toward them. His giant belly bouncing like a whale that had been given legs. The three women saw him and panicked. It was like their worst fears come true. Under attack by a foreigner. John K raised his sword and sliced two of the women across the neck. They howled in pain. Then he circled around and, panting from the strain, motioned to the mayor.

Then two of the goons went and finished off the job on the two old women. They sliced off the hands, and went to work on the ladies' abdomen. Dewey watched in horror as the two attacked one woman, letting her companion bleed out next to her. They sliced at her back, hacking at her spine as if it were a tree trunk.

The third woman, however, was still unharmed. John K had left her alone.

The mayor beckoned. "Dewey, it's your turn. You must finish off the remaining lady. Put her out of her misery."

He didn't move.

The mayor came over. "Just swing your weapon down on her neck. She's suffering. There's no way she can understand what's going on. This woman has been senile for years. I know her. She comes by the city office every day. Drives us all crazy. Asking for help with her water bill."

He walked over. It was the old lady from the ATM. The woman who asked him for help. Revulsion gurgled from of his stomach. He felt a metallic taste in the back of his mouth. Running away, he didn't get far before he vomited.

"There, there, Dewey-san," said the mayor. "We need to build you a strong stomach."

"Her family might have abandoned her, but I'm not going to do it. I won't kill her." Dewey dropped the machete at his feet.

46

The three goons ran up to him. "You have to kill her," said one of them, "or we'll tie you up."

"Now, now," said the mayor, "that's no way to treat our honored guest. He's just a bit squeamish at the sight of blood. It's understandable. He's from the city. Doesn't know what it's like to deal with livestock."

"Part of how a government functions is how it deals with those less fortunate," said Dewey. "Killing her won't solve your money problems. Once you're done with the old and the infirm, who's next? The insane? The stupid? Blind people? You can extend your cost saving argument to every member of society."

The mayor shook his head and took the machine gun out of the bag on his back. "This is no time to philosophize. It is time to act." He walked over to the woman, aimed at her head, and fired.

Dewey closed his eyes. He really wanted to cry, but he didn't.

"That was a bullet we didn't have to expend," said the mayor. "This isn't America. We have a limited supply of ammunition, and no way to get more. Also, half the mountain must have heard that gunshot. They will be fleeing from here now, making our job much harder. We will continue, but if you are told to kill, you will kill. Understood?"

"Or what?" said Dewey.

The mayor stayed silent. He wasn't used to his orders being interrogated. It was clear he didn't like Dewey's impertinence. He waved to the goons, and the procession continued on.

"You sure made him angry, buddy," said John K. "Just do what he says. Otherwise, they might try to hurt me. Or kill both of us. You can see how the march is wearing on them. Making it muzukashii for the mayor to make decisions. Don't make this day any harder, will you?"

The mayor waited for Dewey and John K to catch up. "This is part of a tradition that stretches back two centuries. Have you no respect for that? And a far better option than forced suicide. But that is what faces these people. We have no daycare facilities in Kita-Yamanouchi. The government refuses to pay for it. So they have to go to Oga, an hour and a half away. Or be taken care of by their families. What a dilemma. Three hours a day on the road, or being neglected in your final years for a slow death. But you've never considered that, have you?" The mayor turned his back on him.

Daycare. That was the correct word, wasn't it? Back in America, infants were sent to daycare while mommy and daddy went off to work. But in Japan it was expected that women would never consider going back to the job after having a child. Oh, sure, in some wards of Tokyo, government daycare existed. But it was still hard to get on the waiting lists. In Japan you only sent your elderly for daycare, and picked them up at the end of the workday. But now the entire country was moving into Tokyo, old people were left to fend for themselves. Dewey had never seen a retirement home in Japan. He wondered if they even existed.

The mayor turned back to Dewey, still with the angry look on his face. "At least this way," said the mayor, "the able-bodied can still continue to work. Have you no sympathy for them?"

47

The mayor was all over the girl. She was pushing him away, whispering for him to be quiet.

Forty minutes earlier the group had moved off the path and into the forest. The mountain terrain got less steep the higher up they went. That was where they had found a large group of young women, about fifteen or so, walking through the woods. Many of them were the same girls that were at the Irish pub the previous night. They wouldn't say what they were after, and the mayor was not doing much of a job convincing them to explain themselves.

"You're after something? What?"

The girl smiled. "This is our mission. Stay back. You don't need to worry. Go after some of the old ladies further up the path." One of the other girls ran over and whispered in her ear. She beckoned to the rest of the group, who began to walk away without another word.

"Fine," said the mayor, "go on your way. Whatever it is you are doing."

They let the group of women depart without more harassment. But the mayor whispered in the ear of one of the bodyguards, who left to pursue the girls at a discrete distance. Then the mayor turned to the group. "We will rest here for fifteen minutes."

Everyone sat down.

"Be careful where you sit," said John K, "there are all kinds of deadly creatures in these woods."

Dewey had found a log that functioned effectively as a seat. "Like what?"

"Oh, I don't know. Hornets, for one. They've got the craziest types over here. If you get stung, you'll swell up like Popeye. Every year a few people die. One of them flew in the classroom last year at the high school. Every student, all forty of them, fled. I just stood there, wondering what the fuss was about. Then I looked it up later. They're a nasty business. And you got to watch out for wild boar. They'll eat your lunch. Although they won't kill you around here, but down south, in Kyushu, people have died."

Dewey had enough of listening to John K. He moved over to talk to the mayor. "What is going to happen tomorrow?"

"That's the big surprise. I'm sure you will be happy that you are just an observer."

"Why?"

Before the mayor could answer, the goon he'd sent out came back. "There is a group of old men, the fishermen. They're heading down one of the ridges above us."

"Let's go," said the mayor. "Everyone fan out, we don't want them to scatter and escape. Keep Toshi here in sight at all times."

They followed Toshi, the goon in black, further up the mountain. They ascended a ridge that, after a while, headed downwards. Dewey saw there was a break in the trees. He caught sight of the old men.

Then he stopped dead.

At the other side of the clearing stood the group of girls they'd encountered earlier. Except each one of them was completely naked. The group beckoned to the old fishermen, who were practically running to get to them. Dewey found himself getting a rock hard erection. He'd never seen anything like this in his life. Not even at a strip club.

"Stop," yelled one of the girls.

The fishermen came to an abrupt halt. One of the naked women ran to a tree close by. Dewey saw her untie something.

At once, all the old men were captured in a rope net. Where the hell did they get that? Dewey wondered. From the beach, probably. Either way, the old fishermen were trapped, hanging three feet off the ground, in a tangle of bodies.

Soon the net was surrounded by naked women.

With swords.

48

The mayor ran down the hill, screaming. "You've done well. We can take it from here." One of the girls waved her sword at the mayor. He stopped dead. "What are you doing?" he asked.

"Get lost, chikan. Or I'll cut your hands off," she said.

The mayor backed away, caught between staring at the woman's naked body and the weapon before him. "It's against the rules—"

They responded with more swipes of their swords. Dewey saw that each of the dozen or so naked girls had a weapon. Unless the mayor wanted to unleash a hail of bullets, it would be a losing battle for the guys.

"Look, I'm the one in charge in this town. You take orders from me."

Now all of the girls had turned towards him, not one of them flinching in their nakedness. They raised their katanas, and ran towards the mayor. He stumbled backwards, turned around and up the hill. Dewey saw his goons and John K pop their heads up. "Come on," he said, "they've gone crazy. We've got to get out of here. Before they turn their swords on us."

While the rest of the group ran, Dewey stayed at the edge of the hill overlooking the grove where the net had been set up. The lead girl mumbled to the others. One of them saw Dewey and pointed him out. But instead of attacking, the group of girls just laughed, and returned to the net of fishermen. He sat there, watching the scene unfold. A perverse curiosity overtaking him.

The first girl thrust her sword in. A scream of agony came from inside the net. Then another girl plunged in her blade. Then another. One by one they took turns, until one of them yelled something he didn't understand. Their attack became a free for all.

Dewey looked over and saw the mayor by the tree where one of the ropes supporting the net was tied. He was hacking away at it with his machete. Three swings and the rope net came undone. As the mayor and the goons ran off, John K in tow, the fishermen plunged toward the ground. The girls got out of the way at the last minute, barely avoiding being crushed. A bloody mass of old men sprawled out from the net, like serpents rising from a sea of blood. About half of them were injured beyond repair, and lay on the ground moaning, the last bits of their lives slowly draining out.

One of the men ran for the hills. Immediately the entire group chased after him. But there were three others who grabbed the nearest two girls, dragging them away from the rest of the group.

Toward Dewey.

The naked girls struggled. The men ripped their swords away from them. The two women scrambled up the hill, defenseless. One of them tripped, landing right next to Dewey. One of the three fishermen, despite having a face lacerated and bloody, was quick. Already he was almost on top of her. Raising the katana blade over his head, he swung it down on the woman's body.

Dewey reached over and pulled the naked girl away from the man at the last minute. The sword swung into the dirt. She smiled, clutching him tightly. The rest of the group of girls had reached the escaped old men, who were now outnumbered. The two of them were caught off guard, and got stabbed in the back. Both fell to the ground.

The single remaining old man found himself under attack by all twelve of the women. A dozen blades cut into the guy, slicing and gashing his body. Dewey couldn't tear his eyes away—a dozen women jabbing and slicing a chicken. That's what it looked like. He scrambled up the hill, but turned back to watch the gruesome sight, out of a morbid sense of curiosity.

When the man was satisfactorily dead, the group of naked women dropped their swords and approached Dewey. He looked at their bodies, streaked with blood. Their skin soft and white. Bodies skinny and beautifully formed. Many were small breasted, but not all. All them with unshaven genitalia, as if to scream they were sexually mature women.

They surrounded him, lying down on the ground. "We've never seen a foreigner naked before," said the girl who he'd pulled from danger. Dewey lay his arms out and let them take off his clothing. Soon he was naked too, his body kissed and groped by the group, each girl taking turns with their mouths and....

49

Dewey had a smile on his face as he walked through the woods. It was all so wrong. How could his mind be so compartmentalized? Never in his life could he have imagined the intermingling of pleasure and death. And he didn't feel bad about it, either. These people were getting to him. Their total disregard for life.

All he wanted to do was sleep. He sat down in the middle of a thicket of bushes. They weren't looking for him now. Maybe he could hide out. For a couple of days. Once night fell he'd go back to the town, to the beach. Swim to the next village, if that was what it took. All he needed to do was lie low.

"You are the foreigner, aren't you?"

Dewey looked up, in despair. He'd just sat down, and already he'd been discovered. How small was this mountain?

He turned around and found a middle-aged woman staring at him. She had been at the ATM yesterday, helping the old senile lady.

"Come with me," she said, "we can give you a cup of tea."

Dewey said nothing, but his cover was blown. He could only hope the mayor wouldn't find him.

He followed the woman up a ridge. Farther up, through dense foliage, came the sound of voices. Dewey saw the steam from the boiler before he saw the encampment. His legs strained as he climbed the steep hill.

Then he saw the women.

Three old ladies were tied down. They were much younger than the woman from the ATM. Maybe, say, in their late sixties. Dewey knew they had much more life left. Killing them was madness. Yet the housewives had set up a particularly awful method of restraint—their heads were placed in a makeshift brace, made from wood and the kind of sturdy collar that whiplash victims were treated with. They were bound at the neck to keep from sitting up, with a kind of dental brace keeping their mouths wide open. Above them was a sluice, with spouts coming off, diverting scalding green tea to their mouths. One of the women had already drowned, her lifeless mouth overflowing with liquid, her lungs probably flooded. The other two women were almost there. A green-tea killing machine.

Another housewife grabbed a ladle and approached the sluice. Filled a cup with tea.

"Here you go," said the woman, smiling and passing it over.

Reluctantly, Dewey took the beverage. This is how it happens. He remembered a Canadian colleague telling him about a famous murder trial in the early nineties. The guy on trial was a serial rapist who self-promoted himself to serial killer after a couple of years. He had started with his wife's sister, before moving on to the local teenage population. Police agreed to let his wife plea-bargain to a lesser charge, then discovered, to their horror, that she had participated in the torture and murder of her own sibling. Even helped film the whole thing. Perhaps Dewey was falling into that very same mental space. Where ghastly acts lost their horror when accompanied by the appreciative nod of an authority figure. And the congratulations of one's peers.

Out of the bushes, John K and the mayor emerged. "There you are. Taking a break."

Dewey looked up. "I'll stay here." Then wander back to town, he thought.

"No," said the mayor. "I want you with us."

"Why? What is so important that you need me?"

"Because I've decided. And that's final."

Dewey had seen this sort of logic before. It was quite a common way of understanding decisions in Japan. Usually, though, the leader makes sure everyone has some input, even if such opinions are ignored. This mayor, however, ran the town like his own fiefdom. Not listening to anyone. Yet he was obsessed with the approval of foreigners. Insecure about allowing this melee to occur. Dewey's presence somehow gave him the energy to let the killing continue. As insane as that sounded. But it was only crazy if you applied logic and reason. In politics much of that was lacking.

The woman took the teacup away, gesturing for him to follow the mayor. The group hiked up the mountain until they came to a spot on the top of a cliff. It had a spectacular view of the ocean and Kita-Yamanouchi, even better than down below. But it was a long way down if you fell. They were careful as they got to the top of the path.

The first person Dewey saw was the young woman from the ryokan. Her name was Miki, wasn't it? So you're involved in this, too, he thought to himself.

The mayor pointed to an elderly couple tied up by the edge of the cliff. Dewey walked over. It was the man and woman who owned the hotel.

"Are these her parents?" asked the mayor.

Dewey nodded. "She worked there. So I guess she's the daughter. I don't ask for I.D. from the people who serve me breakfast."

"Good." He gestured to one of his black-garbed goons. "Give her the hanko. He grabbed a machete lying on the ground. Now Dewey, you are to kill them."

"And if I refuse?"

"We'll push you over the cliff."

50

Everyone was laughing.

"No," said the mayor. "I joke with you. But you must kill them. Some of us do not trust you to run off on your own. Do this, and all our doubts will be laid to rest."

"If they die," said Miki, "I'll get the hotel. But I can only transfer the documents with their hanko."

That was the standard method of doing business in Japan. Hanko. A personal seal. No one signed anything. Dewey found it odd. All that power in a stamp. They had to be registered at city hall. You could buy hankos for everyday use for a dollar at any convenience store, provided your family name was Japanese. Compared to Americans, people in Japan have a far narrower variety of surnames, since they weren't commonly used until the nineteenth century. For foreigners, you'd have to shell out thirty bucks to get one custom made. Most people had an expensive stamp kept in a safe for major transactions, like contracts or selling your house. Using a cheaper one with a different style of engraving for everyday office use. But if the expensive one ever got taken, you'd be fucked. This had happened to an Italian guy Dewey had chatted with in a bar one night. His vengeful Japanese soon-to-be-ex-wife had taken his hanko and transferred the ownership of their restaurant to her name. And what could he do? Lawsuits can take a decade or more in the Japanese legal system.

Dewey shook his head at Miki. "You don't give a shit about anything, do you? This is all about the money. To take over the family business. And get out of taking care of your parents. Because you know how much work that is. How it will crimp your social life."

"Dewey, take this," said the mayor, handing him a machete, "and don't make trouble like you did the last time."

The weapon was heavy in his hand. He walked over to the couple. They were panic stricken. Even from three feet away, he could smell the booze off them. They had gotten drunk, because they knew their daughter was coming after them. It was the most depressing thing Dewey had ever seen.

"No," he said. "I'm not going to get involved in some sort of family affair." He turned to the daughter. "Can't you see what's going on? The groupthink? They've brainwashed you."

"Oh, yeah?" said Miki. "You have no idea what they want me to do. Go to Tokyo and work in a hostess bar. Or do something worse. Earn money to buy the hotel off them. That's what they want. I want to live and have kids here. Not in some shoebox apartment in Chiba." She lowered her voice and approached Dewey. "What if I told you that the man over there isn't my real father? Or that he raped me countless times as a child? Sneaking into my bedroom. My mother must have known. But she kept her mouth shut. Just to keep the business going peacefully. How would you feel?"

"I stopped feeling back at the edge of town." Dewey dropped the machete. "This is wrong. And I'm not going to kill them."

The girl took the mayor's machine gun. "How do I fire this?"

The mayor showed her how to unlatch the safety. "And just one bullet per person, so aim carefully."

Miki walked over and aimed the gun at her mother's head. Relaxed. And fired. Then repeated for her father. She leaned down to check if they were breathing. "There. All dead."

Something snapped inside of Dewey. This wasn't going to end on this mountaintop. The murder was an endless cycle. They'd broken their promises at every turn. He was going to be killed if he did nothing. If things got rough, he'd be the first to be sacrificed. He had to show them he was dangerous, so that they'd fear him.

Dewey walked over to Miki, who smiled at him. He raised his arm and brought the blade down on her neck.

Miki's head barely made a noise when it hit the ground.

51

You are a fool!" screamed the mayor. "An inhumane person without a conscience. We live in a society with rules. And no one with the yellow arm band was to be killed today."

"You let those girls be attacked by the fishermen—"

"But I didn't kill them."

Dewey was completely covered in blood. The girl, in her last moments, had spurted all over him. The mayor had run and tried to put a tourniquet on her neck, but the wound was too deep. Even the goon squad was shocked by Dewey's savage action.

He slammed his fist into the mayor's throat. The guy doubled over in agony. A gurgling sound came out of his mouth. For a moment Dewey wondered if he'd mortally wounded him. Then the mayor kicked him in the shin, hard.

Dewey's right leg exploded in pain. He felt rough hands grip him as one of the goons flung his body back. The wind was knocked out of him.

The mayor stood up. He was breathing heavily, but otherwise okay. The goons conversed with him in Japanese.

"No," said the mayor. "The elders will deal with him tomorrow."

John K approached, bending over Dewey like a doctor attending a patient.

"Why do they keep talking about tomorrow?" asked Dewey.

"I don't know, buddy. But you really fucked up. How could you do that?"

"Excuse me? Everyone else here has killed someone today. And enjoyed it."

"But we've followed the rules."

"Oh, yeah, just like the Geneva fucking convention, right?"

Before John K could answer, two of the goons dragged Dewey to the ground, wrapping ropes around him.

"I warned you, didn't I? Not to make them angry? They control everything around here. It's their territory. This is going to be the last day of your life, so enjoy it."

There was some shouting from the bushes. One of the goons, Dewey presumed, had been sent out to scout.

The man emerged from the foliage. "We've found the old people's field. The real one this time, taped off with instructions and supplies."

52

The parking lot was deserted. Little more than a gravel patch on the side of the road, dug deep into the mountains. Megumi grabbed the tent from the trunk. As she ripped open the cardboard box, an instruction sheet floated to the ground. She stuffed it in her pocket, just in case it was needed when they got to the lake. She had never assembled one of these before. It was her first time camping.

They lugged down their backpacks. Bibi dragged a cooler of food with large hind wheels on it. Something that had cost quite a bit but was useful in Japan. The tents weighed down Megumi and Bibi's backpacks. They had taken sympathy on Yuko, with her tiny frame. Dewey would definitely be doing the heavy lifting on the way back.

As was common in Japan, the path was well worn down. Yuko had attached a bell to her backpack, a warning to any black bears in the area. She went first, leading them down the slope to the lake. At points the path got rocky, slowing their march for Bibi's cooler. Nonetheless, they made good time. Getting there would be a pleasure, getting out would be hell.

The campsite was also deserted. Which, to Megumi, was everyone else's loss. The area was stunningly beautiful. She dropped her pack and wandered to the lake. The beach was sandy, the result of some long lost nearby volcano most likely. The lake water was perfectly clear. Looking around in each direction, she could see no sign of human encroachment. This might have been the first time in Japan she'd been to a place like this.

The girls plopped their backpacks on the ground. After a cursory look around, they decided to pitch their tents near a well-worn fire pit behind a clump of trees. "They'll work well as a wind break," said Bibi. "I read that it can still get cold at night this time of year."

Two tents were unrolled. The assembly was difficult, the other girls thankful that Megumi had decided not to discard the directions. The bright red tents were larger than Megumi had expected. "We can fit all three of us in one," she said.

"Yeah," said Bibi, "we can leave the other one for food and clothing. Dewey can sleep there when he arrives."

"You want him to be eaten by bears," said Yuko, which produced a chuckle.

Once they were settled in, Bibi took out her phone. Held it up in the air. "I've got a signal...and...it's gone."

Yuko took out her mobile, confirming Bibi's observation. "It must be the mountains. No one lives out here."

"And what if we got injured?"

"Every year many people get stuck on mountaintops. Especially in Nagano."

Bibi couldn't help but grin. "Really? I thought there were trains everywhere."

Yuko slapped her playfully. "Not outside of Tokyo. Every year they have to send a helicopter to rescue people. Usually university students. I knew a Canadian teacher this happened to. She went hiking with a friend, and they kept walking after sunset. They both fell into a ravine, but they survived. Her friend broke her arm. They were lucky to find a road, and a truck driver rescued them."

"That's awful."

Megumi joined them, in her bathing suit. "Are we going swimming?"

Bibi laughed. "I suppose we'd better before the sun goes down."

Megumi waded into the lake, felt the cold water against her skin. It was wonderful and peaceful. The complete opposite of the beach at Enoshima, where crowds of young men constantly eyeballed you. The lake had a gradual drop off. She bent down, feeling the sting of the uncomfortably cold water on her upper body. Sliding lower, she allowed herself to be submerged. It felt great. She swam twenty meters down the beach, then back to the campground. It was so nice to be away from people, from crowds. Living in Tokyo was a strange experience. Despite the lack of crime and the immense convenience of it all, Megumi felt it was necessary to get out every three or four months. The stress built up in you. One year she had stayed there for the obon vacation, and had felt miserable for a month afterward. No, she thought, you had to get out.

Bibi splashed by her and went right in, the water enveloping her body. Two seconds later she started screaming. "It's so cold." Her entire body shivered. Then, once acclimatized, she started swimming. Yuko waded in a bit, sitting down in the sand, but keeping her abdomen above water. Megumi floated on her back, looking up at the sky. So clear. And blue. It was only interrupted by the call of her bladder. She swam back to shore and toweled off.

Megumi wandered to the edge of the campground, but found no public bathroom. So that was why it was deserted. Beyond the fire pits, there were no facilities whatsoever. She grabbed the toilet paper and stripped off her bathing suit, going au natural. But what to do with the paper?

After finding a solution that involved a lot of digging, Megumi went back to the beach. Did some more wading in the water. As the sun got low, she gathered kindling and helped Bibi make a fire.

Yuko boiled a large pot of ramen noodles and let them cool down for half an hour. Then she got the unagi they'd bought in Sendai out of the cooler. On three plastic plates she prepared a dinner of salad, noodles, and eel. Megumi ate it up. It was perfect. The girls made conversation about national parks. But when Yuko had to explain something in Japanese, Bibi wandered off.

Yuko and Megumi did the dishes. When Bibi didn't return, Megumi announced she'd go look for her. She was a bit pissed that the Swedish girl had left all the cleaning to them. What were they? Her servants?

She moved up the hill, passing through a clump of trees. She saw Bibi standing atop a high cliff, overlooking the lake. Below was rock, about a fifty-meter drop off. Bibi hadn't seen Megumi. For a moment she was overwhelmed by a need to push the Swedish girl off the ledge. She had stolen her boyfriend. Made her miserable. Now Megumi could exact revenge. There was no way she could survive the fall. No one would know. Yuko didn't see it. Bibi would be permanently incapacitated. Probably killed. They would go, search for her body. Megumi would lead Yuko in the wrong direction. The next day they could report Bibi missing. It could take days to find her. If the fall didn't kill her, the dehydration might.

But what was the point? She didn't miss Toshi. And killing Bibi would do nothing to make her life better.

Instead, Megumi went back to the campsite and unfurled her sleeping bag.

53

The mayor had gone first, like some general in a ragtag army. Their group had grown, to more than twenty people. The story of Dewey's aggression had spread quickly. They moved slowly through the forest, trying not to alert any elderly to their presence. The mayor wanted to pick off as many of them as possible before they arrived at the safe area.

They must have been close to the top of the mountain when they heard the drumming. Like you'd hear coming from a temple on New Year's Day. The group headed in the direction of the sound. From a distance Dewey saw the forest open up to a wide field. Filled with people and tents. They moved to the edge of the woods.

Smoke drifted through the trees. Campfires surrounded by elderly people. It was crowded. People were standing wherever they could find room. In the glow of the fires you could see the outlines of people entering large tents, others lined up to get inside and rest. In the middle of it all several fires were set up. People gathered round them, taking plates of noodles from old women who Dewey guessed were in charge of the cooking.

The mayor locked the safety on his machine gun and handed it to John K. "There may be stragglers. Pick them off, but don't waste any bullets. And keep an eye on Dewey."

One of the goons took the length of rope he was holding and tied it around what looked to Dewey like a spruce tree. The Japanese contingent departed, leaving John K and Dewey alone.

Dewey sat down, in the dirt at the base of the tree. "Those are some brave people, giving you a gun. Is it because you're from some redneck part of Texas that they think you can shoot?"

"El Paso isn't redneck. East Texas, now that's full of rednecks. You may not believe this, but before I got fat, I was a sniper in the marines."

"You're joking."

"No sir. Took out combatants in Kabul. You're talking to a man with a long list of confirmed kills." John K turned his head. Something had got his attention. Dewey saw it too. An old man had gone to the bathroom in the comforting privacy of a group of trees. John K raised the machine gun.

The bullet cracked the air. The old man didn't flinch at first. Didn't want to interrupt his piss, probably. Then he looked down and felt his waist. Dewey saw the look of confusion on his face as he dropped to the ground.

The drumming stopped. The old people in the field had heard the gunfire.

A group came forward. Right to the edge of the trees. Pointed out Dewey and John K. Gawking at the foreigners with their weapon. As more people came out of their tents, Dewey shook his head. There must have been hundreds of elderly, all moving towards them. They lined up at the edge of the field, their faces scowled with hatred. The foreigners were taking shots at their ilk. Dewey shut his eyes. One of them started shouting a laundry list of complaints about white people. Then more joined in. It became a cacophony.

Thousands of people. Screaming for them to die.

54

Eventually the old people tired out. The yelling and screaming stopped. They went back to their tents. For all their rage, they didn't cross the invisible boundary between the woods and the field. No matter how many bullets John K had in his clip, he couldn't have taken out the entire group. But the question was, who would've gotten hit? They were miles from a hospital, the mayor had said. Kita-Yamanouchi only had a clinic, and the doctor was on vacation. If you got shot up on the mountain, it could be days before you reached a hospital, with the cave collapse and all. There was no way to phone in a helicopter, either.

Dewey took a nap. He had nothing else to do in the late afternoon heat. When he awoke, he saw John K patrolling the woods back and forth. Like a sentry in some obese redneck army. Had he really been a cop at one time? Perhaps. That meant that he could run, despite all that weight on him. But why had he gone along with this crazed scheme? Was it because he slept with underage girls? How could the endgame to this exercise be any better than a Japanese prison? Of course, you couldn't put an entire town on trial. No one goes to jail for a mass atrocity, only for acting alone.

John K was getting worried. Dewey could see it. "You're afraid they're going to kill you soon, aren't you?"

"I don't need to hear from the likes of you, buddy. You've done enough talking today."

"And you've remained silent. Why?"

"It's not important."

Dewey couldn't help but grin. "You didn't expect this. Every part of you thought they'd respect you. Being a foreigner, and all. But you know now that all those people in that field are coming to get you."

John K didn't respond. Just continued to pace back and forth.

There were still a few rays of sunlight peeking through the trees when the mayor returned. "The camp is ready. Dinner has been prepared." He motioned to one of the goons, who untied Dewey from the tree.

The group walked around the field, which Dewey suspected was the top of the mountain. After getting on the main path, the mayor led them to an area where every flat space between the trees was occupied by tents, enough to hold two or three people.

All of the tents looked the same—a bright red plastic, the kind Dewey imagined might be used for mountain climbing emergencies. Or some other official use, like at sea. Each had a picnic cooler nearby. Many of them had garbage strewn about. Dewey watched the ground, not wanting to step in any place used as a makeshift latrine.

"You're destroying the environment of a national park, you know," Dewey yelled up to the mayor. "Haven't you ever heard of ecology? Think of the things you're doing to this mountain. And the forest. All the disease from dead bodies."

No one responded. They were too tired and hungry.

Every two minutes they passed another tent with people moaning or screaming. Making love. Others were eating dinner. Some praying. The forest opened up to a small clearing where every available space had been set up for large communal shelter. Small, command post-style awnings had been set up in a circle, a bonfire burning brightly in the center. Each of the awnings connected to larger tents, identical to the ones put up by the elderly.

"Here," said the mayor, pointing to some cushions, "sit down."

Bento boxes of gyuudon were passed around. They'd turned the mountains into a goddamn Yoshinoya, thought Dewey as he ate the meal of sliced beef and rice. Everyone in the mayor's group sat in a circle around the bonfire.

"What are you going to do to me?" asked Dewey.

The mayor laughed. "Nothing. We'll have to tie you up, because you are a danger to others. We will let the elderly take care of you tomorrow."

"I don't understand."

"You will," said the mayor. "Soon enough."

After dinner one of the goons was handed the machine gun. Led Dewey away. In a direction where few tents had been set up because of a steep incline. The guard allowed him to take a piss, then tied him to a tree. Dewey sat down and closed his eyes. There was nothing he could do now except convince the man watching him he wasn't a threat. The rope they'd tied him up with was less than five or six millimeters thick. They hadn't come prepared to take prisoners. They only had one gun. Dewey could use the bark to cut through the rope, but it wouldn't work if the goon in black was watching.

Dewey could only hope the man would get bored and wander away. It was his only chance for escape.

55

The moon was up, illuminating the landscape. They must have planned it like this. They wanted everybody to be on vacation. The only people left behind would be those that couldn't afford to go anywhere, thought Dewey. Anybody who could get out, had gotten out. Like that woman who'd nearly run him over the night before. This must be some sort of economic contest. Where they had the poor people fight it out. Get rid of grandma, and not have to worry about a whole set of bills and responsibilities. Maybe they would even keep the old lady's social security cheques. Dewey had heard of that. The government still sending a monthly pension payment to people over a hundred and thirty years old. Almost every other week he turned on the news and saw police discovering another mummified elderly corpse. Always arresting a relative who had access to the bank account. In some cases they were still living in the next room. It was like that Alfred Hitchcock movie, except Anthony Perkins wasn't a homicidal maniac, he was just aging and unemployed.

Dewey was awoken by a girl squealing in Japanese. He looked over. Some young woman had brought food to his guard. They were talking. It looked like the guard was doing his best to charm the girl, and she was taking it all in. Punctuating her responses with squeals of excitement. Once the guy finished his gyuudon, he took the girl's hand. Leaned in and kissed her. She giggled. Dewey kept his eyes shut as he heard the two get up. The guard walked by him, then said something to the girl about being able to take a break for a couple of minutes. Dewey could hear their footsteps fade into the background. A few minutes later he heard the girl moaning and screaming. They were making love.

Dewey didn't have much time. Slowly he'd managed to saw through the rope, about halfway, using the tree bark. He sped up the rubbing motion, keeping the material taught with his hands.

The rope snapped free. This was it! He wanted to jump for joy, but he kept quiet. Undoing the rope carefully and keeping low to the ground, he moved away. The benefit of the full moon went both ways. He maneuvered through the bushes, keeping silent. Moving up the hill he passed by a scattering of tents. The mountain began to slope down as the tents thinned out. Ahead of him was a steep incline. Leading to a path away from the campsite. Down the other side of the mountain, or so it seemed.

He kept on the trail for a few minutes. When he'd gotten a safe distance, he took out his phone. Checked the compass. He was heading west. Good. Away from the coast. He was going downhill. The map loaded up, even without internet access. A leftover from when he'd checked it earlier. It looked like he was on the correct route to the lake. This was the very mountain he and the girls had planned to hike two days from now. At least, Dewey was pretty sure this was the right path. It should lead to a narrow bridge. The mountain lake fed into the ocean through a narrow river. Protected by high cliffs. But Dewey and Bibi had selected the campsite for this trail, and the footbridge that spanned the river canyon.

The path opened up. A few steps further on, he heard voices. Dewey decided it was best to keep close to the edge of the trees. Rounding a corner he found himself in sight of the bridge. Carefully guarded by at least ten goons, all dressed in black.

It was hopeless.

There was no way for Dewey to fight his way through the group. He moved off to the side to get a better view. His foot slipped, but he managed to regain his balance. Glancing over, he saw he'd wandered to the obscured edge of the cliff. It was two hundred feet straight down. To rocks.

Dewey gave up on the bridge. He wandered through the woods until the terrain began to slope down. After five minutes of following the edge, he came to a path. Carefully and slowly he advanced. The glimmer of moonlight off the water to guide him. A moment later he stopped and sat down on a large boulder. He'd been going non-stop for half an hour. Would they have noticed he was gone? Probably. They were on their way here most likely. After catching his breath, he decided it was best to keep going.

The path continued, winding its way down. The lake disappeared behind clumps of foliage only to reappear a few steps later. The ground leveled out, but as it did the moonlight disappeared, blocked by a canopy of trees. Dewey fumbled forward, until the glimmer of the water came back into view.

The beach was right in front of him. He moved in the direction of the water's edge.

The cliffs boomed with the sound of gunfire.

Dewey staggered back as the sand exploded, just meters in front of him. He fell back into the foliage. Looking up, his view was blocked by a rocky overhang. He heard yelling. The mayor's voice, shouting instructions. More gunfire. This time further down the beach, and into the water. They hadn't seen him. Good. But they would be coming down here. They must have known he'd head for the bridge.

Dewey dropped his cell phone and wallet in the woods. Moved towards the water. As quietly as possible he walked into the lake, clamping his mouth shut from the sting of the chilly water. Fully submerged, he started to swim to the other side.

56

The lake must drain into the ocean. Why else would he have been pulled by a current towards the mouth of the river? Dewey had caught sight of a glimmering light on the other side of the lake. He couldn't tell if it was a campfire or a streetlight. Stupidly he had decided to swim for it, despite the current pulling him away. His arms exhausted, he was treading water as he was pulled towards the cliffs that marked the start of the river. He swam harder, moving towards the far rocks. The river wasn't wide, but the current was getting stronger. When he could bear it no more he felt himself going under.

This was it. Death.

His feet hit the lake bottom. Shore was close. This energized one last burst of his dying muscles. He was dragged into the mouth of the river, but it was shallow. He pulled himself onto a large wet boulder. Gasping for breath. For the first time he looked up at the sky.

He was directly under the bridge. A bad spot. The moment he caught his breath he moved again, dragging himself along the rock walls of the ravine. Soon he was back out into the lake. But it was still rough going. With no beach in sight, just solid rock.

Dewey swam, his muscles sore with exhaustion. When he could bear it no more he pulled himself up against the rocks. Once he stopped panting, he continued on. The light on the shore was a constant, and it was getting bigger. Ten more minutes of pulling himself along the cliff walls continued, until he reached a flat beach. He got up out of the water, and walked towards the flicker of light. It was close enough that Dewey was sure it was a campfire.

When he got to the fire, it was Bibi that saw him first. She reacted with fear, until she saw his face. "Dewey?"

Yuko and Megumi turned around, shocked.

Dewey sat down by the fire to warm up. He was shaking with chill. "Something terrible has happened. We have to get out of here. Now."

"What?" said Yuko.

He explained the events of the last twelve hours. Yuko translated for Megumi.

"This is insane," said Bibi, "you don't expect us to believe—"

"Are your phones working?"

"Intermittently, but—"

"We have to phone the police. Now."

"Are you crazy?" said Megumi. "The government would never do such a thing. You have been eating mushrooms from the forest."

"I didn't swim through the dark just to get your sympathy. Or if I did, then I've gone insane. Either way you should phone the police."

Yuko tried her cell. "No signal. It only worked briefly this afternoon."

"Do you have a car?"

"Yes," said Bibi, "but it's a half hour walk away. Uphill."

"We have to go. Now. Our lives are in danger."

No one moved.

Dewey turned to Bibi. "Can you smell alcohol off my breath?"

Bibi leaned in. "No, you're sober."

"So why would I do this? We've got to get out of here. They know I've escaped. They're coming. And they've probably seen your campfire, too."

Yuko and Megumi chatted in Japanese. Megumi kept shaking her head, but finally relented.

"Maybe you were injured swimming in the lake," said Yuko. "We'll take you to a hospital. Tomorrow we'll buy you dry clothes. But it's dark, and we forgot to buy flashlights."

"If we don't go, they'll kill you," said Dewey.

Minutes later, they left.

The hike was grueling. Uphill the whole way, and shrouded by a canopy of trees that obscured the moonlight. The path had just begun to level off when Megumi screamed in terror at the back of their line. Dewey whipped around.

"I've stepped in mud," she yelled in English.

It was true. As she climbed back up onto the path, her lower half was drenched. She had stumbled into a patch of swamp on the side of the path.

"You'll be okay," said Dewey. "Stay close."

"We're almost there," said Bibi.

The car was just up ahead. But something caught Dewey's eye. Something moving. He pulled on Bibi's arm. "Did you hear anything, in those bushes?"

"No, why?"

"Just a feeling."

"And a good feeling it is," came the mayor's voice. He emerged from the forest, surrounded by a dozen goons. "You girls should put more trust in your friend Dewey."

57

"Tonight we have discovered an uncomfortable truth," said the mayor. "That the list of innocent people we have to eliminate has grown. It is not a task that I relish. In fact, we will all be severely punished by the government."

Dewey started to laugh. "You must be joking."

"Not at all," said the mayor. "Our group has trespassed on the grounds of a national park. This is a great infraction."

Dewey was about to respond when he noticed a rush of motion beside the mayor.

Megumi plunged through the goons and grabbed the machine gun. The shock on their faces. They never expected a girl to take charge like this. She ripped the gun out of the mayor's hands and fired. The goon nearby took a bullet to the head, an explosion of blood landing on the car's windshield.

Next to him, a second bullet deflected off the bumper and impacted another goon's leg, causing him to howl in pain.

Dewey punched the guy beside him as hard as he could. The man uttered a winded grunt, then doubled over. Almost instantly Dewey felt himself pulled to his right, and tilted upside down. Yuko and Bibi joined the melee, attacking the three other yakuza. The mayor backed off.

Megumi held up the gun, shouting orders. The men stopped fighting, and regrouped around the mayor. Megumi yelled to Yuko, who went and opened the trunk of the rental car. Got out a spool of rope.

"What's that?" said Dewey.

"We bought it at Tokyu Hands in Sendai yesterday," said Bibi. "In case we had to hang the food from tree branches. To keep away the bears."

Dewey moved over to help Yuko when he caught a glimpse of movement. Coming from the path that led to the lake.

Out of nowhere came another group of goons, five or six. One of them grabbed Megumi, another wrestled the gun out of her hands. Megumi's fingers depressed the trigger. Bullets sprayed into the sky. The magazine was exhausted in a dozen seconds, or less. The threat of death gone, the goon dragged Megumi toward him, knocking the butt of the weapon against her chin. She howled in pain, and immediately had three men on top of her.

The mayor shouted orders at the goon with the gun. He tried to check the magazine, but only touched it briefly. "Too hot," he said, the only words Dewey caught.

The mayor barked more orders. The goons divided into two groups. One to tie up Dewey and the girls, the other to siphon gasoline out of the rental car's tank, which they did by jacking up the rear and knocking out part of the gas tank with a wrench from the emergency kit in the trunk. One of them had ripped the upholstery off the seats, and used it as a sheet to capture the leaked gasoline, pulling it out and spraying the exterior of the vehicle, then placing the sheet back under the tank to gather more accelerant. By the looks of it, Dewey assumed they'd done this before.

Once they were tied up, the group moved to the far side of the parking area. The machine gun had cooled enough to check the magazine. The mayor wasn't happy. "Well," he said, "that's all our ammunition. I hope you're happy now. We would have killed you quickly. But this won't be the case." The mayor walked over and grabbed the hand of one of his goons, helping him to his feet. "We were doing you a favor."

"You're completely fucking crazy," said Dewey.

One of the goons got out a lighter and lit a dried leaf on fire. Then placed it gently on the car, which erupted in an inferno.

Bibi looked at the flames pouring over the windshield. "Well, at least it was only a rental."

The goons tied their arms and legs with rope. Not tight enough to prevent them from walking, but just enough to slow them down. Which, on a narrow mountain path in the middle of the night, was all the confinement they needed. Then the group set out.

58

"You have to find a way out of this," Megumi whispered in Bibi's ear.

"Why me?"

"Because this trip was your idea."

"It was Dewey that got me to go. We're all in this together."

Bibi felt someone stroking her hair. She turned around and saw it was the mayor. "Quit it."

"I was only admiring you," he said. "We don't see many blond girls in these parts. The last one was a JET in the late nineties. But she went back to Scotland." He put down his hands. "You should be careful."

"Why?"

"Many of the men around here are perverts. They will not treat you well. I can try to defend your honor, but I will also be busy defending my own life."

"I don't understand."

The mayor yelled up to one of his goons leading the pack. The procession came to a halt. "Let's rest here before we cross the bridge."

They paused and sat down. Everyone was exhausted. It was slow going in the dark, and the hike from the car had been mostly uphill. Dewey knew that it would be even steeper after the bridge. He watched as the mayor sat down next to Bibi. Felt a pang of jealousy.

"So you see, Miss Bibi, today we have been killing as many of our elderly as possible. They are not allowed to fight back. They can only hide, or shelter in a field at the top of the mountain. But tomorrow, the tables are turned. They are allowed to kill the adults below the age of sixty. And we are not allowed to fight back. Nor can we use weapons. There is also the fact that we are outnumbered."

"By how many?" asked Bibi.

"Easily four or five to one," said Dewey.

"The only way to survive is to get back to the town of Kita-Yamanouchi. That is our safe area. We begin the march again at dawn. So you see, searching for you is robbing us of precious time."

"Then why don't you have it at night?" asked Bibi. A perfectly obvious question.

"Too dangerous," said the mayor. "Someone could get injured. Or fall off a cliff."

The mayor got up to talk to some of the guards sitting on the other side of the path.

"It makes total sense," said Bibi, once the mayor was out of earshot.

"How?" said Dewey.

"I once read this article. About people who attempted suicide and failed. One of the men they interviewed jumped off the Golden Gate Bridge, in San Francisco. And survived."

"Wow."

"It was his second attempt. The first time he walked up on the west side of the bridge, but he wanted to jump off the east railing."

"Why?"

"I have no idea. Maybe he wanted to see the city lights as he fell. Anyway, he didn't jump the first time because the traffic was moving too fast for him to cross. He was afraid to get hit by a car."

"But he was heading to...."

"I know. But the metal state of people about to commit suicide often doesn't make sense. The same thing is going on here. Except we're watching it happen to an entire society."

"Like Jonestown."

"Where?"

"You know, Jim Jones. French Guyana, 1978."

"I don't know who that is," said Bibi. "But, back to the suicide survivors, the journalist asked them if they'd do it again, and every one of them said no. The guy who jumped off the Golden Gate Bridge? As he was plummeting to the water, he realized that he had made a very bad decision. Like a moment of clarity when your life is really threatened. The same thing will happen with these people."

"Maybe," said Dewey. "The only question is, will they have that moment before they kill all of us?"

59

That was why all the fucking. All those people. Might be their last night on earth. That was what Dewey was thinking as their prisoner procession was led up the mountain, back to the camp. In total darkness. They had been caught up in something unimaginable. Now it was unlikely that any of them would survive.

The mayor directed them to the outskirts of the encampment. Their legs were bound, but not tightly. Dewey didn't complain. The goons would depart soon enough. Then he and the rest of the girls would make a run for it. Head as far as possible down the mountain. And hide. All in different places. Make it difficult for them all to be found.

The lead goon stopped at a tent, a large one, which could easily house five or six people. "Inside." They complied. The interior was lit with a small battery-powered lamp. The goon zipped up the front flap.

Dewey looked over at Megumi. "Thank you for that."

"For what?"

"Trying to take their gun."

"Lots of good it did."

Yuko looked terrified. "Are we going to die?"

"No, I doubt it," said Dewey. "He just wanted to scare us."

Everyone lay down on the hard cold ground. They didn't have sleeping bags.

Dewey leaned over to Bibi. "The only way out is by water," he whispered. "As far as I know."

"How can we get back to the town? There's an entire mountain…."

"It's all downhill from this point. If we can spread out—"

Dewey was interrupted by goons in black ripping the door to the tent open. They reached in and dragged Bibi by the legs. She started to scream. "No," yelled Dewey, "take me, instead. I got her into this."

The goons stopped and looked at each other, puzzled. They hadn't expected a protest. For a moment they murmured to each other, then one of them took off, in search of higher authority.

Minutes passed in awkward silence. Then the goon returned. He beckoned to Dewey. "Come."

"All of us will go."

Megumi and Yuko, who seemed to be in some kind of shock, came to life, following Bibi and Dewey out of the tent. The goon led them to the old people's safe ground.

At the edge of the field was an old man. It took Dewey a couple of minutes to recognize his face. He was the guy from the beach. With the daughter kidnapped by the North Koreans. The man looked at Dewey. "We regret you got involved in this. There was…a bureaucratic mistake. With the hotel registry."

"Leave the girls alone. Take me instead."

"I'm afraid this is bigger than all of us. Your friend, the Swedish girl, she will be sacrificed. There are no other options."

The goons dragged Bibi away. She screamed. One of the men covered her mouth. A moment later she was gone, vanished into the dark forest. Dewey made a break to go after her, but was clobbered by four goons. They marched him back to the tent in silence.

Once inside, he sat in the corner, shivering in the cold. The Japanese girls chatted in whispers. At one point Yuko broke down in tears. Dewey was too exhausted to muster his second language skills. Half an hour later some yelling erupted outside. The mayor came into the tent, sat down. Someone handed him bowls of a steaming liquid. "This is from the old people. They are very sorry that you got caught up in all of this." Food was passed over to Yuko and Megumi. The mayor took some, too. "Please, begin."

Dewey took a spoon and dug into the contents of his bowl. It was a warm watery rice concoction. Okayuu, he thought it might be called.

"This is a tragedy," said the mayor. "You might survive tomorrow, but it is unlikely that I will."

Dewey felt tired and closed his eyes. The okayuu….

Megumi and Yuko were already asleep.

They had been poisoned, thought Dewey, just before he lapsed into unconsciousness.

60

The earth was rumbling. Waves of vibrations passed through the ground under the tent. Dewey awoke, peeking outside. It was still pitch dark. He checked Yuko's phone. Five-thirty. Twenty minutes until sunrise. He'd never felt an earthquake while camping. Or even at ground level. It must have been a big one.

He listened carefully. No one was stirring. He undid the ropes around his ankles. Unzipped the front of the tent.

Outside the sky was starting to get light. He ran over to a tree and took a piss. His head stung, and he still felt sleepy. He looked around. Toward the area where the camp had been set up the night before.

Everyone was gone. Nothing was left but the smoldering embers of a fire pit.

Then he heard it. The drumming. The chanting. They would be coming. Soon.

He got closer to the field where the old people were camped out. Watched as they performed some kind of ceremony. It was sacred and terrifying at the same time. The sun would be up soon. They had to leave. There were thousands of elderly. All with murder on their minds.

Dewey got back in the tent and shook Megumi. She stirred slightly. "Come on, we've got to go." What was he going to do if they didn't wake up? They must have been given the same amount of sleeping medication, but Dewey, with his larger body, had processed it quicker.

Megumi bolted up, like she was hit with an electric shock. She fell forward. Behind her someone had tried to stick a katana into the tent. They bolted for the exit.

As they pulled themselves outside, they were surrounded by five old men. Only one had a sword.

The sun was up. Time to kill.

Megumi wrestled with the swordsman as Dewey was dragged away by the other four elderly. He got about fifty feet from the tent when he saw Megumi flip the swordsman. She ran towards him, weapon in hand.

The four old men were now tired out. Dewey landed a karate kick against one. He was a terrible fighter, but he was still stronger than this bunch. The tallest of which was a full head shorter than him. They hadn't prepared for this. Perhaps they thought everyone was playing by the rules. Megumi came up and sliced them at the back of their knees. They howled in pain and fell to the ground.

"You're good at this."

"My father made me practice as a child."

"Is your back okay?"

"Yes, but...." Megumi saw something over his shoulder. Dewey spun around in the direction of the tent.

Yuko!

A crowd of elderly people had it surrounded. When they saw Dewey coming toward them, the entire group grabbed the tent and dragged it away, back in the direction of the field.

Megumi screamed, and grabbed Dewey's arm. "We have to go."

He looked back. Hundreds of old people were coming over the ridge.

"Come on," said Megumi. "There is nothing we can do for Yuko."

The two ran like hell down the mountain. They reached a small cliff. Megumi jumped first, followed by Dewey. They smashed through bushes and trees. They passed a clump of cedars and the ground went vertical. Dewey tumbled with her down the slope, falling through the brush. They came to land in a clump of spruce trees.

Dewey stood up. He was dirty, covered with leaves and mud, but nothing was broken. Just a couple of scratches on his hands. He turned to Megumi. "Are you okay?"

She got to her feet. "I think so." The sword had also survived the fall. She grabbed it and started to walk away. "Let's go."

"They're not going to follow us over that slope."

"Yuko is dead. We will be next, if we don't get to the town. Let's go."

Dewey shook his head. Shocked by her coldness. But his head was swimming. This was not the time to argue.

They pushed their way through the trees. It was tough going. Lots of dead branches and sticks. They weren't even out of it when they saw the tape, fluttering in the breeze.

61

Dewey hadn't seen a cassette tape in twenty years. He remembered a group of kids, the bad kids, from his elementary school. They'd gotten hold of a Pearl Jam album. Smashed it on a rock. Ripped out the narrow chestnut colored spools of magnetic tape.

Megumi held her sword high, looking out for old people ready to attack.

"Maybe we should follow this," said Dewey.

"Why?"

"It might lead us to Bibi."

"She is dead, Dewey."

He turned to her. "Look, you can go. Run away, to the town. But I'm not giving up on our friends. Not until I'm sure we can't help them."

She stood there not moving.

"Well," he said, "why are you bothering to stay with me?"

"Because you know the route back to town."

Her logic was impeccable. She needed him. For the moment.

They followed the streams of tape. As they moved down the mountain the tape got thicker and thicker, like some kind of garish tinsel decorating the trees.

After a couple of minutes following the magnetic tape, they heard a loudspeaker. A voice. Soon Dewey realized it was in English. Followed by Japanese. Listening materials for an English lesson.

Megumi put her hand up. "Look."

Dewey turned to his right. Through a clump of trees he saw some old ladies. Around them were giant piles of tape. They were wrapping something. They must have broken hundreds of cassettes to get enough to cover up the thing, splayed across a table. With a heave, the women lifted the object up.

It was John K. Wrapped in audiotape. Like a mummy. Around his neck a noose had been woven from the same material he was wrapped in. Tied around a nearby tree.

One of the ladies screamed. Belted out something in Japanese Dewey didn't catch.

"What did she say?"

"She said, this will be the last time you correct our English mistakes. Her family made her take English lessons, to get her out of the house. So the family had a break from taking care of her. And she hated it. Every second."

The women, about a dozen or so, tried to lift John K up onto a stool. He thrashed around like a wild animal, but two of them kept him in place with katana swords. The noose held loose against his throat. Hanging down from a thick tree branch.

The old ladies pulled the stool away. John K dropped. Even from a distance, Dewey could hear a nasty cracking sound. John K's body hung from the tree, lifeless.

The old women bowed to the corpse and smiled at each other. Turned off the tape recorder. Together they walked away. When they were out of sight, Megumi and Dewey approached.

Dewey looked up at John K's lifeless body. "The man was scum. But he didn't deserve to die so senselessly."

"We should go," said Megumi. "This could be a trap. Please show me the way to the town."

"Sure," said Dewey, "but can we cut him down?"

"We don't have time."

"But—"

From far off in the woods came a scream.

"They're killing someone," said Megumi.

"It could be Yuko. We've got to find out."

"There's nothing we can do. They've got her. We have to flee."

"No. If she's alive, we need to try and rescue her. These old people don't have much strength. We can take them."

Megumi shook her head. "We need to get the police. These people are crazy."

"But the government approved this."

"No, the mayor is lying. All of this must have been made up on falsified documents. Japan could never be so... barbaric. Something is wrong here. We have to get help." She started to walk away. Dewey followed.

62

They didn't get far before they heard the scream again.

The men were trying to pull the mayor apart, limb by limb. But their hands kept slipping. Dewey and Megumi watched from the bushes. Shocked by the savagery of it all. But as gruesome as it was, Dewey felt no remorse. The mayor was tied down on the ground while they pulled. But, despite the screaming, the mayor was still very much intact. The men tugged. The mayor screamed. Until he passed out.

A new group of old men arrived, all of them dressed in suits. It was completely surreal. Business attire in this environment. The old men dragging at the mayor's appendages stopped. Conversed with the suits. Then each of the half-dozen or so businessmen took off their ties. Tied them to the mayor's arms, legs and neck. Each of the ten or so men took up a position.

Roughly two on each tie. On the count of three they began to pull, like a grotesque game of tug-of-war.

The left leg came clean off. The two men pulling were flung backwards. Blood spurted onto them from the exposed femoral artery.

Then the mayor's head came clean off. Something in the tie, maybe a piece of wire, or some kind of ultra-strong fabric, had severed the neck. Blood everywhere, it was a huge mess.

The men relaxed for a few minutes. Some wiped the blood off themselves. Their job done, they continued down the mountain.

When they were gone Dewey walked out. For a moment he looked at the scene of carnage. After watching John K, it felt like the wellspring of revulsion had run dry.

Megumi shook her head. "Let's go."

Something caught his eye. "Look," said Dewey, "over by the far trees—"

"What?"

"A sword. I want to get it. Can you come with me?"

"We should go."

"I want a weapon."

They walked over to the sword. But halfway there, Dewey heard something spring. Rope. Below them the ground flew up. Megumi's katana flew out of her hand.

Caught in a net. Like the old fishermen the day before.

Out of the woods came a group of old people. Laughing and jeering. The old men examined Megumi. Some tried to grab at her body, even through the netting. To them, she was the real prize.

The yelling calmed down as a procession of elderly appeared through the trees. Carrying something.

Only once they got close did Dewey catch sight of Yuko.

63

Megumi had to pee really bad. Ever since she'd left the tent. In the mayhem of the last half hour she'd forgotten about it. But now that her body was upside down, her bladder had changed the angle at which it cried to be relived.

She looked down at Yuko. Still asleep. Lucky her. They had laid her out on the ground for everyone to see.

For Megumi it would a terrible death. She knew that for sure. The best she could do was hold her bladder, waiting to release it on her unsuspecting captors. Even if she couldn't fight back, she could resist to the last. Watch their surprised faces as piss dribbled down their cheeks.

The fisherman grabbed a squid. It was giant. He had kept it in a large square aquarium that took an entire group to lift. Its flesh was purple and pink. Megumi recognized it immediately.

The umaziki puffer squid. It was common in the seas around Kyushu, especially near Miyazaki. Something that could be deadly. The creature could latch onto your face. Using a giant vacuole, it could suck the air out of your lungs, causing them to collapse. Suffocation was inevitable within a minute. That's what made the animal so dangerous.

The fisherman lay it gently against Yuko's face. Tentacles flew everywhere. Above its beak and beady eyes, the skin expanded like a balloon. Yuko came to life, struggling to get it off. Megumi shut her eyes. Her coworker didn't have long to live. Soon it would be Dewey and Megumi's turn. At least suffocation is better than bleeding to death.

Most of the men moved on, leaving a small group of four. One of them, who had spoken to Dewey at the top of the mountain, approached. The one who had declared Bibi's fate. He unzipped his pants, shoving his crotch at Megumi's face. She looked at his limp dick and burst out laughing. It was the only way to deal with her fear. "Look at you. Can't even get it up, eh?"

The man growled. Turned around to the group of men. "Where's Takeshima? He has the chousen ninjin pills."

Ah, thought Megumi. Korean ginseng extract. For erectile dysfunction. These men would know it well.

The man ran off, the rest of the group following. One of them looked back at her. "We'll gang-bang you, you eikaiwa bitch."

Now they were alone. Dewey was talking to her in English. He wanted to know what the men wanted. She told him they were angry about Yuko putting up a fight. No need for him to know how dirty these old men are.

"Do you have your cell phone?" asked Dewey.

She felt around. From one of her Velcro pockets she produced it. "What are you doing? There is no signal."

"I'm going to smash it."

At first Megumi thought about stopping him, but resisted the urge. The device was useless if she was dead. He took out his belt. Used the metal catch to smash the glass screen. Used the glass shards to saw through the net.

It took time, but Dewey managed to cut a hole. He tumbled out. Megumi followed behind. Dewey looked around and took her hand.

They ran. Megumi didn't even look back at Yuko's lifeless body.

It was half an hour before they stumbled upon Bibi.

64

The butter. The first thing Dewey saw was the butter. He and Megumi had burrowed themselves in a clump of spruce trees. They looked out on the setup the old ladies had used the previous day for making tea. The boiler was steaming away, but the sluice wasn't producing hot water. It was melting butter. Old ladies loading huge buckets of it onto a hot metal plate. The smell was what had attracted Megumi and Dewey's attention in the first place. On their way down the mountain. Dewey had thought they might be able to pick up a couple of useful weapons.

He never expected...this.

The sluice had run melted butter into Bibi's mouth. For, it seemed, quite some time now. The butter was flowing right down her throat, her lips and teeth held open by a nightmarish dental contraption, her nose pinched closed.

The body.

The body had bloated. Like a corpse.

But it was still alive.

The arms.

The legs.

Were gone.

Burgundy splotches where limbs had been.

The stomach rose.

Bibi was breathing.

Living through this torture.

Her body had bloated to five or six times normal human size.

"We have to kill her," he said. "Give me the sword"

"Wait," said Megumi. "People are coming."

It was a group of old people, led by the gentleman Dewey had met on the beach. The man was spouting out Japanese so fast Dewey couldn't keep up.

Megumi ducked down, dragging Dewey with her. "If they see us, were dead."

"I can't watch this go on. Just let me go over there and cut her throat. Let her bleed to death. She'll pass out from the shock."

"Don't move," said Megumi. "I'm trying to hear this. They're talking about the adults. They haven't got most of them. Many people have escaped from the mountain. The old people are angry. That man, he's really angry. Killing Bibi is taking too long."

But Dewey was barely listening. For the first time since he was a child, Dewey found himself fighting back tears. If he did start to weep, their position would be given away.

Women arrived at the scene. Began to pour ice over Bibi.

"What are they doing?" he asked.

"They're trying to cool Bibi's body down. They want the butter inside her to cool, causing her to burst."

"These people are sadistic."

"This is Japan. In the countryside."

More yelling erupted from the group. The man from the beach broke away. Katana sword in hand. Ran over to Bibi.

The katana blade came down, cutting the air with an odd howl. Bibi's head rolled across the ground. Decapitated. Dewey used every muscle in his body to keep from bursting out of the trees. Attacking the guy. He had put on such a display of kindness. But he was a monster. Maybe North Korea was his excuse. But it was no reason, in Dewey's mind, to justify this. He must think all foreigners are against him, doesn't he?

Megumi tugged at Dewey's shirt. "We must go. Now."

65

Dewey and Megumi raced down the mountain, all kinds of horrorshow on display around them. The hills were alive with the act of death. Every ten meters groups of elderly were busy attacking the slow and the invalid of the adult population of Kita-Yamanouchi. They flew through the trees.

Megumi screamed.

Dewey looked over.

The goons, still in black, tied up with white rope, all lined up for the slaughter.

Each head lopped off by a sword.

Each screaming in terror.

"Come on," said Dewey, dragging her away.

Then the thundering started. The vibrations of feet heading down the mountain. The heavy breathing. And growling in pain.

THE TWO DAY MARCH

The crowd was streaming down the hill. Some carried pitchforks; others with kine, the mallets used to pound mochi. Thousands of them pursuing. A race to the bottom. Some of the elderly stumbled and fell in the stampede. All slow moving. All determined to kill.

Dewey and Megumi hid behind a clump of trees.

One of the men blew an antler-shaped bugle. The horn's notes signaled the crowd to stop. There was much yelling. Dewey heard the word foreigner. Looked up and saw an old man screaming orders, pointing in his and Megumi's direction.

They took off, running fast, avoiding trees. It didn't take long. The trees parted. A view stretching to the ocean appeared.

Then the stench. Dewey would never be able to forget it.

He saw the old couple's bodies, decaying and covered with flies. The ones that owned the hotel. And nearby, the daughter. They'd been left to rot in the sun.

Megumi stared at them. It was finally becoming clear to her. The face of death.

She stood there, petrified.

66

The pause was all it took. Dewey and Megumi were surrounded. They watched as masses of old people hobbled down the hill. Each of them with a weapon. There was nothing they could do now.

Dewey turned to Megumi. "It's been nice knowing you. I hope we really get the chance to—"

The mountain began to shake. Far worse than the earthquake earlier that morning. Megumi clutched Dewey's torso as he desperately tried to steady himself. He flailed, gripping a skinny thread of a bush, the only thing his hand could grab on to.

All the old people stopped, terrified expressions on their faces. Wave after wave pulsed through the ground, each more violent than the next.

A giant crack, like thunder, cut through the air. Everything below Dewey's feet disappeared. He was falling. Wrapping his arms around Megumi, he shut his eyes. "Hold on tight," he screamed.

Dewey slid with the ground collapsing around him. He rolled end over end. His nostrils were plugged up with the stink of raw earth. They were falling down a river of mud and soil. When the ground leveled off, more dirt piled on top of him.

He lie there, clutching Megumi, feeling like a corpse buried alive. The shaking stopped.

Dewey dug himself out of the dirt and mud. Megumi was next to him. "Are you okay?"

"I think so," she said.

He sat up, and looked around. A huge part of the mountain had collapsed. But the mud had been soft enough to break their fall. All around them were uprooted trees. They had landed near a small lake, which extended underneath a cliff.

From the nearby bushes a deer emerged. Walked all the way over to Megumi's feet. Began to nibble on a berry bush that had been dislocated.

"Not afraid of humans, are they?"

"Just like Nara," she said.

It was like they'd landed in some heavenly paradise. Much nicer than the rest of the mountain. This lasted barely a moment before Dewey heard shouting. He looked around. At the top of the cliff. Where they had been before the landslide. A crowd of people had gathered. Pointing to them. Some were already trying to climb down.

"Don't these people ever give up?" he said. "Come on, let's go."

They beat through the bush, moving down the mountain as fast as possible.

"Is it much farther?" she asked.

"No, we're almost there. Once we get to the town, they can't hurt us. We've got to hurry." They burst through some bushes and found the path back down. Picking up speed, they ran as fast as they could. Dewey caught sight of the lookout point, where he'd stopped with John K and the mayor on the way up. The final leg of the journey. No one chasing them. Such luck.

Then came the sound of a whip. Dewey and Megumi were knocked off their feet. Into a net. Covering them like jungle animals.

"Don't move, foreigner," said an accented voice.

"Are you okay?" he asked Megumi.

"Yes," she said.

Dewey managed to clear the net off his head. To see themselves surrounded by old people, weapons at the ready.

"What do we do now?" asked Megumi.

"We die."

67

Dewey and Megumi had been dragged to the edge of the cliff. Below them the drop off ended in solid granite. Tumbling head first, the chances of survival looked to be pretty much zero. If they did stay alive after the impact, most likely they'd be left there. Without medical attention. If they were found, it would be days or weeks from now.

Behind them, the slope of the mountain created a natural amphitheatre. For the elderly citizens of Kita-Yamanouchi to watch as the death sentence was carried out. Like in the old west, coming out to watch a hanging in the town square.

Through the crowds that surrounded Dewey and Megumi appeared the Shinto priest. The one Dewey had seen at the beginning of the two day march.

Megumi hissed at him, and began shouting. Dewey didn't catch a word of it, but he well imagined what she was saying. "How can you do this?" he said, when Megumi stopped screaming. "What's the point? You've killed pretty much everyone else of consequence. Even the mayor. What is accomplished by killing an innocent girl, who had no intention of getting caught up in this?"

"It is punishment," said the priest. "For the lack of respect you give our customs. You come here. Think we are like the rest of Japan. Here to obey you, the American. This is not Tokyo."

"What is he saying?" said Megumi.

"I don't know. Did you learn the word 'bullshit' in your English class?"

She slapped him on the arm.

The Shinto priest produced a scroll. He began to chant. In the ancient impregnable Japanese that was used at weddings. Today...used for a death ceremony.

Dewey turned away, looking out at the town below. People were running away from the mountain, streaming towards civilization. They had been the people who had left the mountaintop encampment early. Successfully outrunning the elderly. How many were there? Maybe six, seven hundred. Or more. All the adults of Kita-Yamanouchi, or at least most of them. Reunited with the town's children. So unfair that they would escape, but Dewey and Megumi were to lose their lives. It didn't make any sense. Then again, how could any kind of mass killing be anything but batshit crazy? Even with all the murder during the first day of the march, most of the old people, or at least several hundred, were still alive.

A siren pierced the air. Even at the great distance away on the mountain, the sound carried from the center of the town. Dewey hadn't realized how silent the forest had become. Ever since the earthquake.

Something was happening down below. Small dots of people were running into the street. From the houses. Running towards the mountain. Some of them reached the edge of town, but still far from the start of the path leading upwards. They were at least half a kilometer away.

Then Dewey saw the wave.

It was hard to see, at first. Just a giant grey line, growing on the ocean horizon. But he knew it didn't look right. The thing sucked the blue from the sea. It just grew. Small waves hit the breakwater, near the train station. Overflowing.

The Shinto priest stopped his chant. Walked closer to the edge of the cliff. "What is…this?"

One of the old people started screaming. Dewey only picked out one word: tsunami.

"It has come," Dewey said to Megumi.

"Yes."

He could see the boats being knocked around, bounced onto the shore, like toys. The waves enveloped the beach, then the breakwater, streaming over the town.

Then Dewey saw the ship. It arrived out of nowhere, hidden by the mountains to the right of his field of vision. "Oh…my god."

An oil tanker.

It slammed against the edge of the cliff that nestled the north side of Kita-Yamanouchi. The vessel snapped apart, spilling its black contents, mixing with the seawater, creating a grey nastiness. Then came the sound of an explosion. The ship disappeared in a giant fireball. Flames stretched out, flowing over the waves.

The sea.

The sea was on fire.

Screams erupted from the elderly on the hill. They began to flee, together, up the mountain.

Dewey watched as the steep cliffs around Kita-Yamanouchi funneled the wave and the fire. The people below were crushed as the waves overtook them.

A moment later everything was engulfed. A sea of flame heading for the mountain.

68

In the end, the forest didn't burn down. Not the whole thing. A fire that had burned away the foliage at the lower elevations had been stopped by a late-morning thunderstorm, and the moisture left in the vegetation. As night fell, Dewey and Megumi walked back to the lake with the deer. Dewey had crafted a shelter out of tree branches and leaves. They had found a leftover picnic cooler with bottled water and snacks, settling in for a long uncomfortable night. There was no sign of the elderly of Kita-Yamanouchi.

The next day they hiked down to the town, just after dawn. The outside world had discovered the carnage. Two coast guard ships were anchored off the shore. Helicopters surveyed the damage. Dewey suspected the old people were already burying the dead on the mountain, covering up the evidence of the two day march. They walked through the smoldering remains of the lower slope of the forest.

By the time they got to sea level, Dewey saw the water had receded, leaving the land with a coating of mud and sewage. The oil had all burned off before it could ignite the ruins of the town's buildings. Wood was everywhere, reduced to kindling. A few roofs and plumbing fixtures stood intact, but that was about it. In the remains of the train station lie the wrecked halves of the oil tanker.

For a while, Dewey and Megumi stood at the edge of the destruction, stopped in silence. Then elderly people appeared, crying and screaming, streaming past them. Looking for the remains of their houses. Dewey felt a sense of pity as the people moved past. For all the things they'd done to him and his friends, they didn't deserve this.

Helicopters started to land, with rescue supplies. The man with the clipboard appeared again. Dewey remembered him from the previous day, shouting out population figures. Just before the start of the march. One of the rescuers approached him. They talked. Dewey walked over to hear the conversation. Megumi followed, too.

"Total number of survivors, Kita-Yamanouchi," he yelled over the roar of the helicopter blades, "young people, under twenty, zero. Adults, two. Elderly over age sixty, one thousand five hundred twenty-one." The man turned to Dewey. "The tunnel to Oga has been opened. Please go to the entrance. A bus will arrive shortly."

Dewey, speechless, walked away. Towards the remains of the town. Megumi followed. They were dirty, tired, and desperate. Numb from the events of the past twenty-four hours.

As they walked through the ruins of the wrecked town, something caught Dewey's eye. Under a roof that remained intact. Something pink.

"Wait," he told Megumi.

Dewey approached the object. It was a child's toy. A Care Bear. He remembered the cartoon from his childhood. Reaching down, he tried to pull it free. The stuffed bear was stuck. With all his strength he leaned down and gripped. With a mighty heave he pried it away. Nearly falling over backwards. When he regained his balance he examined the toy. It was almost in perfect condition. Then his eyes glanced to the ground, settling on where he had ripped it loose. He crouched down. In the mud he saw a child's hand. Clean as if it had just been washed. Reaching up from the rubble.

Dewey wept.

Don't miss the next chapter in
The Tsunami Trilogy

The Summer That Shivered

Turn the page for a preview of
The Summer That Shivered…

猿も木から落ちる。
Even monkeys fall from trees

—Japanese proverb

An Introduction of Sorts:
What is a MicroSievert?

Saturday, March 12, 2011

The worst part of an earthquake is not what you see in movies or on TV. People say how they saw this building collapse. Or they saw people drown. Or some other horrifying image. But that isn't the case. The worst thing about surviving an earthquake is the shivering.

What's that, you ask? Well, I don't really know much about it either. Basically, after a big earthquake hits, your body retains a sense memory. It's not retained in your conscious mind, perhaps not even in your brain. More like a physical memory embedded into the fibers of your nervous system. When you're drifting off to sleep or just taking a nap and your body is jolted awake. It feels like the entire room is shaking. Adrenaline is pumping. Muscles are clenched. The body is preparing a fight or flight response. The building could be collapsing around you.

And it's all a lie. Your body is lying to you.

It's not paranoia. Or fear. Nor anxiety. It's something physical, something left over from our ancestors, a dormant relic of an ancient animal nervous system, useless to us modern humans. Except for those who live in a country like Japan.

That's were I was. I was walking from my shoebox apartment to Ebisu station. Ebisu is a part of Tokyo. Some people think it's a really rich part. A good theory, except that I live there.

Today I got to the station, feeling lucky that the trains were actually running. Everyone in the Tokyo area lives and dies by the trains. Imagine if all the gas stations ran dry in Los Angeles. Or everyone in New York lost their shoes, all at once. That is what Tokyo is like without the trains running. At the ticket gate I stopped and glanced at what was on the monitor above the collector's booth. It was news footage from a helicopter. An entire commuter train. Near Sendai. Overturned in a rice field, like a toy. I found out later it had been evacuated before the tsunami hit. Symbolic of what had been going on for the last 24 hours.

I went to go meet JB, a friend of mine from university. He's got a pretty sweet position. He's a scientist. And makes almost twice the money I do, except he doesn't have to pay tax. Which is like making four times what I make. He works hard, though. I don't.

We were sitting at The Hub. Getting drinks. Talking about our experiences. When he went to the washroom I lit a cigarette. The earthquake news was on the projection TV. I can read and understand Japanese, a rare thing for most white people in Tokyo. The news in Japan is always subtitled with a near-identical transcription of the audio. It's hard to keep up with the kanji. Then I saw a katakana word I've never seen before. Micro-something. Micro-what?

JB came back. He's a scientist. He knows shit like this. "What's a microsievert?"

"No idea," he said, gulping his beer. "It's not my field of expertise." He took notice of the TV. "What are they talking about?"

"I don't know. It's a lot of science kanji. Something about an explosion. Just before four o'clock." The image changed to a map. "It's something about the nuclear plants. There's three of them in trouble. One in Aomori, and two in Fukushima."

"Where's Fukushima?"

I wracked my brain. "I passed through it a couple times on my way to Hokkaido. There's nothing there. Unless you're going skiing. I doubt the snow's very good, though. Too far south. Too close to the ocean. It's north of here, before you get to Sendai."

It was happy hour, so we continued drinking. You can probably fill in the gaps for the rest of the story. I won't bore you with the details. You might think I'm a total narcissist. I don't really care. I wrote this for myself, so feel free to move on to some other book. Or website. This is a journey through a part of my life in the twilight of my twenties. I don't want to give away the ending, but it turns out I live. Despite all I've been through.

I want to give you all some context for this story. Let me outline for you the seven stages of a single man's existence. Number one: pre-pubescence. From childhood to the end of high school. Your body develops and you experiment, trying to meet girls. Hopefully figuring out what works, at least some of the time. You're limited by the fact most people live with their parents. Young men fumble around, hopefully getting laid. Hopefully not getting anyone pregnant. I've had both success and crisis in those fields. Most young men are terrible at sex. And young women say, boy, you're terrible at sex. Young women talk about emotions and feelings. But the truth is they're not very good at sex, either. Most of them. But that's okay.

If you're part of the lucky 20% who go to university, you get to...go to university. And what you do for four years doesn't matter. Unless you're going to be a scientist or a doctor or a lawyer. Or an engineer. Or a grad student. Who really cares about getting good marks? You just got to pass that shit. It's all about the piece of paper. Most of your time is spent screwing around. Even if you do become an engineer.

There are lots of people who meet someone in university. Back in the day that was the person you married. Thus ensuring the continuity of the upper middle class lifestyle. But that's not where I went. Post-school, I didn't have a job. I joined the creative class. That means you're unemployed a lot. I don't mind being without a job, but it requires a certain kind of personality. This leads to stage three: post-school. Most men hit their peak here. They may have a girlfriend, some might get married. Some come out of the closet. But we're mainly concerned with the swinging bachelor. The man with the apartment, the car, the tie. The money comes in. But there are no kids to suck it out of your bank account. If a guy cheats on his girlfriend and she doesn't find out, nobody cares. No financial slash legal consequences. And if she breaks up with you, there are usually other girls around, anyway.

After that comes marriage. Unless you don't settle down. In which case this leads to what I call "optional extras". Stage four is the adventurer phase, but we'll get back to that. Stage five is the "everyone else is getting married" phase. Men value their freedom. But, in their heart of hearts, they know being alone isn't so great. Men get older, and they want someone by their side. This phase used to hit younger, with society and economic pressures and all that. Nowadays by your mid-thirties you've got to ask some questions. Am I making enough money? Am I hideously ugly? A loser? By 40, a lot of men feel the need to get their act together.

There's a sixth stage. If you don't get married, you often still make a lot of money. And are able to live well. There are those poor saps you know—friends in a relationship with a woman who gave birth. This means they might not have sex for a year. Not you, though. Then there's your buddy's self-sacrifice. And crying children in the middle of the night. Daycare bills subsuming the down payment on a sports car. The single man sees this and says "I'm successful at my job, so screw everybody else." Or else, he's in prison. Locked up with the rest of the 1% who don't play by the rules. Either way, who cares? No meaningful relationship, but no hassles.

This leads to the seventh and final stage, which I call "the Scotch years." It's the stage of life I fear the most. In more primitive eras this was the domain of men who wanted to marry other men, but weren't allowed. Or they were sailors. Or the crew of the starship Enterprise. My only direct experience with this stage came in high school. I had to take an overnight train from Moncton to Montreal. This was back in the days when the East coast trains had couchettes. Basically a private room with a fold out bed. They were amazing. I remember smoking a lot of hash in one of these compartments....

But I digress. As I boarded the train, I passed one of these compartments. There was an old man, sitting down. Looking out the window. To his left was a nearly full bottle of scotch. His nourishment for the next fourteen hours. My image of stage seven bachelorhood. Was he happy? Who knows? I never talked to him. At some point having everything to yourself gets boring. So I guess you end up becoming a drunk.

The story that follows is squarely in stage four. It's adventure. I guess. But this isn't a travelogue. It's a story, and not a very good one. Happy moments are boring, so I've tried to cut most of them out. Oh, and there's a lot of sex, too. So you shouldn't really read any further. It might make you angry. Don't blame me. All I did was write it down, so don't bitch and moan. And don't think I published excerpts from my diary without cleaning up the really naughty parts. Trust me when I say, what you're reading is the sanitized version. All tidied up for public consumption. The truth is far, far worse.

Since this story takes place in Japan, there's a lot of strange vocabulary, places, and cultural concepts. Most of them I didn't bother to explain. This diary is bloated enough as it is, but I've put in a glossary at the end. Peruse it at your own risk; I don't claim to be an expert.

And one last thing. I subtitled this book "A Diary of blah, blah, blah, in contemporary Japan." That means my contemporary, not yours. So take every bit of information on the pages that follow with a grain of salt. Most likely, it'll be ancient history by the time you get around to reading it. Oh, and one more thing: these journals were originally recorded as audio files on my Japanese cell phone. Some of the date stamps got corrupted when I transferred them over to my computer. 99% of the dates are correct. But if you notice a mistake, don't fret too much. I never let accuracy get in the way of a good story.

Now onward.

Part One:
Without a Clue or a Condom

Saturday, June 16, 2007

Why did you come to Japan?

That's the most common question I'm asked. And every single time I don't know what to say. It's complicated, really. The answer people want to hear is "I came here for [whatever] reason." They want something simple. But moving from one country to another is complicated. Unless it's for a vacation or a brief work stint, it never has a simple explanation.

The problem is I'm from Canada. If I was from, say, Guinea-Bissau, no one would bother asking. The answer is obvious. One country is super poor. The other is not. In Japan these questions come loaded with the whole inferiority-superiority complex. People wonder why you'd come to Japan if your country is so great. But then, Japanese people always want you to praise their country. Which you do. At first. Most people from English speaking countries come to Japan with very high expectations. However, like a supermodel who farts in your bed, reality is usually less than ideal. But you can't say that because people get all upset.

For the record, these are the reasons:

1. I wanted to live overseas. It was at the time in my life when I figured a move would be least damaging to my long-term career prospects.

2. To learn a foreign language (namely, Japanese). Explore a foreign culture (ditto). And travel to exotic places.

3. To sleep with foreign girls. Japanese girls are fine, but I don't discriminate.

4. To eat wonderful foreign cuisine. Canadian food is, well...what is Canadian food, anyway? Besides donair poutine?

5. To find adventure.

Those are the main reasons. I'm sure there are others. The point I'm making is that I've been asked this question by almost every person in Japan. It makes me feel sympathy for celebrities. They have the same problem—everyone asks you the exact same question. Every time. Always. The first few times you don't mind. But after 10,000 times it gets annoying. You start getting pissed the moment you see the word being formed in their mouths. You want to change the subject. Hopefully you get past this stage. Learn to take such interrogation gracefully, otherwise you risk spending the rest of your life as an asshole.

The third question people would ask, after "Do you like Japanese girls?" is usually "Do you like living in [wherever city/town/mountain village this is] ?"

Now, I live in Tokyo, which is an unusual place. Even by Japanese standards. People here have a reputation for being cold. I mean, people are the same everywhere. But it's at work where a lot of people in Japan turn monstrous. And petty. It might be a hangover from Samurai times. Or it may be due to the fact there's no functioning legal system here. Once the police decide to arrest you, it's pretty much case closed. Suing is astronomically expensive, and the justice system works slowly. Back home a case taking years is unfathomable. You could have killed someone. Trial not speedy enough? You can walk free. In Japan, however, legal time is measured in decades. But yeah, sure, on paper, it's very similar to North America.

Now, I'm a foreigner, so people tend to treat me as an exception. Which is both good and bad. There are a lot of people in Japan who have way worse lives than I do. Like people who work in restaurants. That's a truly shitty existence. And a huge part of Japanese culture is food. At least I don't have to work a fifteen-hour day. That's what I was doing back home, before I left.

And among Asian countries Japan is probably the best place to work. At least I'm not working in some factory in China.

Thursday, July 5, 2007

The first place I lived when I came to Japan was a town called Chigasaki. It's a suburb of Tokyo, an hour by train from Shinjuku station. It's nice, quaint. It's famous for being on a major train route, the Tokkaido line. It's also close to the beach. I thought it was okay, but I only stayed for three months.

The first week I was there, I decided to go to a bar. I found this tiny, hole-in-the-wall establishment. A "snack" bar—one of many in the area. Inside there were three men, an extra seat, and two weathered-looking women. There was some karaoke equipment in the back.

I sat down. One of the women was talkative. She started to speak to me in English.

"Do you know what kind of bar this is?" asked the bartender, putting down a small bowl of potato salad.

I nodded. Obviously snack bar meant they served you small snacks with your drinks. So I bought a drink. Had some conversation with the other men and the girl. I think we talked about geishas at one point. Kyoto is the place for that kind of thing. Then I left. I didn't feel like making conversation.

Later I found out a "snack bar" in Japan is where men go to drink and talk to girls. Or ladies. The place I went was pretty typical—two or three girls, with seats for three or four customers. Usually they charge quite the fee in addition to the drinks. I suppose the bartender realized right away that I was fresh off the boat. He only charged me for the drink.

After that I found an English-style pub. The first time I was there I talked with a cop. He complained about the racism he encountered in New Zealand as a university student. I wasn't sure how to react. I'm not from New Zealand, nor was I there in 1988, when he was. What can I say? I don't represent all white people.

To be honest, I wasn't offended. Today I decided to go back. Some guy in a suit came in and bitched me out. He spoke English, but gave the impression he was a yakuza.

"We have been colonized by America," he said.

Uh-huh. I ignored him.

"I'm so drunk," he continued.

I stared at my drink.

"In this bar, we speak Japanese!"

I'd only been in the country for three weeks. Already people are berating me for not being fluent in the language.

"I'm really drunk." The guy downed his drink. "All the people in this bar speak English, perfectly well. We want to speak Japanese!"

Except for me, the bartender and this guy, the bar was now empty. The three other customers had made a beeline for the door as soon as he started. Lovely country, this.

I ignored the guy. He stopped trying to talk to me. I finished my drink and left.

Maybe it was time to find a new place to live.

Friday, August 8, 2008

The letters L and R are really difficult for Japanese speakers. They have a consonant that is almost identical. But the tongue placement is in the middle of the mouth. More than L, but not quite R. It's a bit difficult to master for English speakers. Usually our L sound will suffice. The problem arises with certain Japanese names. Should you pick L or R? That was my problem with Risa. I mean, I could call her Lisa. But she never learned English, and the R is more exotic.

We met when I was still dating Yumi. I had been taking Japanese lessons for six months in Ebisu. I was terrible. No one at work would use anything but English with me. I would have approached people on the street. But, you know, people in Tokyo are weird about white people.

Tokyo is the largest city in the world. It's one of the four alpha cities, along with New York, Paris and London. It's also the only one of the four where it's virtually impossible to find someone fluent in English. Even amongst Asian cities, Tokyo is pretty bad. Nonetheless, Japanese people understand that outside of their country almost nobody speaks their language.

Now, everyone in Japan gets a minimum of six years of English education. Signs and product labels are usually in English and Japanese. It's roughly analogous to the role of French in English Canada, or Spanish in the States. Let me be honest, I have a lot of negative opinions. But generally I'll agree I really have no right to be judgmental. But I can say with authority the English education system in Japan sucks. To be crystal clear, many people in Tokyo seem to have a bit of a superiority complex. They think when they encounter a white person they have to start speaking English. Doesn't matter if the person is Albanian or Bavarian. Unfortunately most people have no conversational ability whatsoever. So you end up facing a person spurting out random English words. All of them completely unconnected by verbs or prepositions.

As you can imagine, this isn't a particularly good environment to learn Japanese. In August, I always got a week and a half of vacation for obon. It's when all Japanese go back to visit the graves of their ancestors and tidy them up. I bought myself a seishin jyuhachi kippu, or a "young person's eighteen" ticket. Basically anyone over eighteen can buy it. You pay about a hundred dollars. For that, you got five days of unlimited travel on all local trains. You can mix and match the days anytime over a three-month period. And you can use it with a friend. The only catch is, you can't take the bullet train or sleeper trains. For me that was fine.

The first day into my August vacation I got up super early in the morning. I took a train from Ebisu all the way to Aomori. Departing at seven-thirty in the morning, I didn't get to the final train station until eleven at night. Along the way I traveled on trains that were shockingly small. After Sendai they literally were two-car country line services. When I got to Aomori I found out I could take a night ferry to Hokkaido. It would save me hours compared to the train—and it only cost fifteen dollars. I bought some beer and grabbed a cab to the ferry terminal.

Aomori is still on the island of Honshu. But the temperature was lower than it was in Tokyo. I had left the stifling summer heat behind. For about two hours I drank myself silly, then crashed on the floor in the second-class compartment. The whole trip from Aomori to Hakodate only took about three and a half hours. When the boat docked I stumbled out into the dawn's light, still drunk. I passed by some girl. She was still asleep on a chair while everybody else disembarked.

"It's time to get off, you know," I said. In what was probably broken Japanese.

She said nothing. Possibly rendered speechless by either my whiteness, or the booze on my breath.

An old man was kind enough to lead me to the JR station nearby. I waited for another hour and a half in the morning heat at the train station. It wasn't so bad compared to Tokyo—the humidity was almost non-existent. Around seven-thirty a single-car train pulled in to the station. Inside, the only air conditioning was the open windows. Within minutes we were out in the countryside. Enveloped by trees. For some context, you must understand that summer in Tokyo is a race between air-conditioned spaces. Leaving a climate controlled environment feels like a risk to life and limb. That is how bad the humidity is. Hokkaido might as well have been on a different planet.

Around nine-thirty the train stopped. The last station on that part of the line. It was a forty-five minute wait for the next departure. I really had to go to the bathroom. Beer will do that to you. The train station bathroom was closed. It felt like I was in the middle of a national park. Nothing would be open until ten, long after the next train had departed. In front of the station was nothing other than a parking lot. And a large expanse of grass with some log-cabin style buildings on the other side. Perhaps the first expanse of grass I'd seen in months. In one of the log cabins I found a bathroom that was open. When I walked back I passed the girl from the ferry.

"There's a washroom in the cabin to the right," I said.

She didn't respond. Maybe my Japanese wasn't so great after all.

The day before I'd spoken to at least three old ladies on the train. They seemed the happiest to talk to me. One woman in Iwate spent over an hour chatting. Explaining how she had gone to watch mochi being made. For the first time in my life I had spoken a foreign language all day long. Not a word of English. So I was plenty happy to talk to this girl. We chatted for a while in the train station. Her name was Lisa. She was a college student from Nagoya.

We traveled together for the next three hours. I told her about Canada. She told me about her university. It wasn't an easy conversation—she didn't speak a word of English. Mostly I nodded and smiled when she spoke. Occasionally I would respond with an "I understand" or "I got it."

After a while we both fell asleep. She leaned into my shoulder. I didn't mind—she was cute. If she wanted to pretend to act like a girlfriend, that was fine. It was rather awkward for a moment when we woke up. Then I just took her hand. Don't ask me why. If you asked me to testify, I couldn't answer. I was guilty of having feelings for a girl I had just met.

We watched the countryside pass by. For some strange reason I was excited like I was thirteen again. A farmer got on near Niseko. He sat down across from us. He took one look, muttered something under his breath, and walked off, looking for another place to sit. Soon after that he returned. In front of me was the only free seat on the train. Me and Risa stopped holding hands.

We got to Sapporo and parted company. I helped carry her bag. She gave me her phone number. I didn't expect to ever see her again. I was just happy to be in a place where it was warm. But not the suicide-inducing swelter of Tokyo in August.

Glossary of Japanese words used in this novel

Author's note: This is a partial list of Japanese terms I've used in this book. With the exception of place names and businesses, Japanese is almost never written in romanized script. Because people are so used to using kanji to recognize vocabulary, writing Japanese words with our alphabet causes a lot of confusion, even for this author. The glossary below should alleviate such ambiguity.

a

Akabane　赤羽 (あかばね) a train station in north Tokyo
Akita-ben　秋田弁 (あきたべん) Akita dialect; "ben" is often used as a prefix
Azubu-Juban　麻布十番 (あざぶじゅうばん) an up-scale neighborhood in central Tokyo

b

Beckers　ベッカーズ a fast food restaurant, similar to McDonald's, run by JR Group, often found in railway stations
Bunkamura　文化村 (ぶんかむら) a multistory complex in Shibuya, Tokyo, with galleries, theaters, restaurants, and an upscale department store

c

CanCam キャンキャン a women's fashion magazine
chikan ちかん pervert; train groper; molester
chousen ninjin 朝鮮人参 (ちょうせんにんじん)
North Korea ginger extract; used to solve erectile
difficulties
chu-hi 酎ハイ (ちゅうはい) a sugary alcoholic
beverage (usually between 4-8%); kind of like alcoholic Sprite, although it sometimes comes in other
flavors
Cinecitta チネチッタ a famous independent movie
theater in Kawasaki

d

Daikanyama 代官山(だいかんやま) a wealthy
neighborhood in Tokyo known for small, fashionable
boutiques
daikon 大根 (だいこん) a kind of near-flavorless
Japanese radish; resembles a large white carrot,
and is often served grated
Dogenzaka 道玄坂 (どうげんざか) an area of
Shibuya with many love hotels
Doutour ドトール a Japanese coffee chain

e

Echizen soba 越前そば (えちぜんそば) buckwheat
noodles famous in Fukui prefecture
eikaiwa 英会話 (えいかいわ) English conversation
school; privately run, many of these are chains
Enoshima 江ノ島 (えのしま) a small beautiful island
off the coast of Shonan beach in Kanagawa prefecture, near Kamakura

f

Futako-Tamagawa 二子玉川 (ふたこたまがわ)
a neighborhood on the western border of Tokyo,
across the Tamagawa River from Kawasaki

g

gaisen uuyoku 街宣右翼 (がいせんうよく) right
wingers, especially those who drive around in black
vans
Gakugei-Daigaku 学芸大学 (がくげいだいがく) a
station in southwest Tokyo
genkan 玄関 (げんかん) entryway or foyer, where
people leave their shoes
genki 元気 (げんき) energetic; used as a greeting
gyuudon 牛丼 (ぎゅうどん) a bowl of rice topped
with shaved beef cooked in sauce

h

Harajuku 原宿 (はらじゅく) neighborhood in central
Tokyo famous for teenagers, cosplay, and cheap
clothing stores
Hachioji 八王子 (はちおうじ) a suburb of Tokyo
near the mountains; generally accepted as the
farthest area west before the Tokyo area turns into
central Japan
hanko 判子 (はんこ) a stamp, always used in Japan
in place of a signature
hiro-no-maru 日の丸 (ひのまる) rising sun emblem
on the Japanese flag
Hiroo 広尾 (ひろお) a wealthy neighborhood home
to many English speaking foreigners

i

Iidabashi　飯田橋（いいだばし）a station in central Tokyo
ika　イカ squid
inaka　田舎（いなか）the countryside; specifically, the area outside the borders of Osaka City and Tokyo's 23 special wards; this definition causes confusion as there is no English translation—for example, Kawasaki, although it is considered inaka, to most English speakers is indistinguishable from Futako-Tamagawa, a Tokyo neighborhood it borders; indeed, this author has even heard Nagoya, a metropolitan area of 9 million people, referred to as 'the countryside'
izakaya　居酒屋（いざかや）a tavern where people sit and order food with their drinks

j

Joetsu　上越（じょうえつ）a city in northwest Japan; the Joetsu bullet train, although named for the city, does not stop here

k

Kabukicho　歌舞伎町（かぶきちょう）love hotel and entertainment district on the east side of Shinjuku station; considered seedy and dangerous
katana　刀（かたな）Japanese sword; illegal to own
kanji　漢字（かんじ）Chinese characters used to write Japanese
Kannai　関内（なんない）a busy, commercial neighborhood in central Yokohama

Kanpachi dori 環八通 (りかんぱちどおり) number 8 of the major ring roads that circle around Tokyo
Kasumigaseki 霞ヶ関 (かすみがせき) a station in central Tokyo famous for government offices
Keihin-Tohouku Line 京浜東北線 (けいひんとうほくせん) a train line that runs from Kanagawa to areas north of Tokyo
kine 杵 (きね) an oversized mallet used for pounding rice to make a glutenous rice paste called moochi
kinshin-kon 近親婚 (きんしんこん) inbred
koban 交番 (こうばん) a small neighborhood police station, usually staffed by one or two officers; if you are lost, you can ask for directions there
Koriyama 郡山 (こおりやま) a city in Fukushima prefecture

l

Lumine ルミネ a department store chain

m

mabou doufu マーボー豆腐 (まーぼーどうふ) tofu in a spicy chili sauce; named after a Chinese dish, but tastes very, very different
Marunochi 丸の内 (まるのうち) the area near Tokyo station; also the name of a subway line
Minato Mirai みなとみらい a futuristically-designed port area of Yokohama with many skyscrapers
miso みそ a bean paste, often used to make soup
Musashi-Urawa 武蔵浦和 (むさしうらわ) a station in Saitama, a northern suburb of Tokyo
muzukashii 難しい (むずかしい) difficult

n

Nambu Line　南武線（なんぶせん）train line in Kawasaki
natto　納豆（なっとう）savory fermented beans,
often eaten with rice for breakfast; has the consis-
tency of melted marshmallows; most people outside
of Eastern Japan consider it disgusting
Nodai　農大（のうだい）nickname for the Tokyo University of Agriculture

o

Ofuna　大船（おおふな）a city in Kanagawa prefecture
Oga　男鹿（おが）a city in Akita prefecture
okayuu　おかゆ watery rice, often served to people
who are sick
okonomiyaki　お好み焼き（おこのみやき）a savory
pancake-like dish, famous in Osaka and Hiroshima
OL　オーエルー office lady; a typical low ranking
clerical position held by young women in Japanese
corporations
Ome　青梅（おうめ）a western suburb of Tokyo
Omotesando Hills　表参道ヒルズ（おもてさんどうひ
るず）a high end shopping complex in central Tokyo;
many mixed use skyscraper complexes in Japan
have the English word "Hills" tacked onto the end
for reasons that make no sense
Onibaba　鬼婆（おにばば）the devil
onigiri　おにぎり a flattened ball of rice, usually
wrapped in a seaweed paper, topped with a variety
of tasty delights
onsen　温泉（おんせん）hot spring

r

ryokan 旅館 (りょかん) a traditional-style Japanese inn, usually in the country; often elaborate multi-course breakfast and dinners are included in the (usually expensive) price

s

Salarymen サラリーマン a male office worker in Japan

Sangenjaya 三軒茶屋 (さんげんぢゃや) a station in western Tokyo; generally considered a nice place to live

seishin jyuuhachi kippu 精神十八切符 (せいしんじゅうはちきっぷ) young person's 18 ticket; allows for unlimited travel over five single days on any local train run by Japan Railways; only available during specific times of year

sen (as in chikan-sen) 線 (せん) prefix meaning train line; Megumi adds the word to 'chikan' to make a joke

Shonan-Shinjuku Line 湘南新宿ライン(しょうなんしんじゅくらいん) an express train that runs from the Pacific coast Tokyo suburbs to Shinjuku

Shimo-Kitazawa 下北沢 (しもきたざわ) a trendy west Tokyo neighborhood; popular with students and people in the film industry

shinkansen 新幹線 (しんかんせん) bullet train

Shin-Koiwa 新小岩 (しんこいわ) a working class neighborhood in east Tokyo

shochu 焼酎 (しょうちゅう) an almost flavor-less clear liquid, not unlike vodka, usually between 20-40% alcohol soapland ソプランド a brothel that involves a lot of fooling around with soap bubbles

Sobu Line 総武線 (そうぶせん) a local train that passes through central Tokyo; it runs parallel to the Chuo Line Rapid Service trains

Suica スイカ watermelon; also the name of a re-chargeable plastic card that can be used to pay train fare

t

tatami 畳 (たたみ) thatched floor mats, often laid down in the room of a home used for sleeping

teppanyaki 鉄板焼き (てっぱんやき) a kind of fry-ing surface used to cook meat and vegetables in front of customers at a table or counter

tomodachi ともだち friend

Toyopet トヨペット a car rental agency run by Toyota

Tsujido 辻堂 (つじどう) a neighborhood of Fujisawa, Kanagawa

u

uchi 内 (うち) inside, innermost; often used as a prefix in place names

umeshuu 梅酒 (うめしゅ) sweet plum wine (~12% ABV); comes in other flavors sometimes

unagi うなぎ broiled eel, covered with a sweet sauce

Uniqlo ユニクロ a store known for cheap, fashion-able clothing

y

yakitori-ya 焼き鳥屋（やきとりや）a restaurant that serves small skewers of barbecued chicken

yama 山（やま）mountain; often used as a prefix in place names

Yamate 山手（やまて）an upscale residential neighborhood of Yokohama

Yokosuka 横須賀（よこすか）a far-flung Tokyo suburb with a large American naval base

Yoshinoya 吉野家 a fast food restaurant famous for gyuudon; popular with salarymen

yukata 浴衣（ゆかた）a garment, often confused with a kimono, worn in the summer; more casual versions are worn like bathrobes; always provided by Japanese hotels

Yurakucho 有楽町（ゆうらくちょう）a station in central Tokyo famous for shopping and theaters

Yurindo 有隣堂（ゆうりんどう）a chain of large bookstores

z

Zainichi 在日（ざいにち）ethnic Koreans who were in Japan, but not considered citizens

About the author

Shane O'Brien MacDonald was born in 1980 on Cape Breton Island in eastern Canada. He speaks English, Japanese, and Chinese, and has a degree in economics and film studies from Queen's University. Before becoming a novelist he worked as an editor, cinematographer, and assistant picture editor on dozens of films and television shows. He has also been a foreign language instructor at the Tokyo University of Agriculture.

Mr. MacDonald is the author of the Kiki Claymore series of books, which have been described as "post-Ian Fleming female-centric espionage comic books in novel form."